TRIPS TO THE MOON
by Lucian

Translated from the Greek by Thomas Francklin, D.D.

Table of Contents

INTRODUCTION..5
INSTRUCTIONS FOR WRITING HISTORY......................................10
THE TRUE HISTORY...28
    BOOK I..28
    PREFACE..29
    BOOK II..42
    ICARO-MENIPPUS. A DIALOGUE..56
NOTES...69

INTRODUCTION.

Lucian, in Greek Loukianos, was a Syrian, born about the year 120 at Samosata, where a bend of the Euphrates brings that river nearest to the borders of Cilicia in Asia Minor. He had in him by nature a quick flow of wit, with a bent towards Greek literature. It was thought at home that he showed as a boy the artist nature by his skill in making little waxen images. An uncle on his mother's side happened to be a sculptor. The home was poor, Lucian would have his bread to earn, and when he was fourteen he was apprenticed to his uncle that he might learn to become a sculptor. Before long, while polishing a marble tablet he pressed on it too heavily and broke it. His uncle thrashed him. Lucian's spirit rebelled, and he went home giving the comic reason that his uncle beat him because jealous of the extraordinary power he showed in his art.

After some debate Lucian abandoned training as a sculptor, studied literature and rhetoric, and qualified himself for the career of an advocate and teacher at a time when rhetoric had still a chief place in the schools. He practised for a short time unsuccessfully at Antioch, and then travelled for the cultivation of his mind in Greece, Italy, and Gaul, making his way by use of his wits, as Goldsmith did long afterwards when he started, at the outset also of his career as a writer, on a grand tour of the continent with nothing in his pocket. Lucian earned as he went by public use of his skill as a rhetorician. His travel was not unlike the modern American lecturing tour, made also for the money it may bring and for the new experience acquired by it.

Lucian stayed long enough in Athens to acquire a mastery of Attic Greek, and his public discourses could not have been without full seasoning of Attic salt. In Italy and Gaul his success brought him money beyond his present needs, and he went back to Samosata, when about forty years old, able to choose and follow his own course in life.

He then ceased to be a professional talker, and became a writer, bold and witty, against everything that seemed to him to want foundation for the honour that it claimed. He attacked the gods of Greece, and the whole system of mythology, when, in its second century, the Christian Church was ready to replace the forms of heathen worship. He laughed at the philosophers, confounding together in one censure deep conviction with shallow convention. His vigorous winnowing sent chaff to the winds, but not without some scattering of wheat. Delight in the power of satire leads always to some excess in its use. But if the power be used honestly—and even if it be used recklessly—no truth can be destroyed. Only the reckless use of it breeds in minds of the feebler sort mere pleasure in ridicule, that weakens them as helpers in the real work of the world, and in that way tends to retard the forward movement. But on the whole, ridicule adds more vigour to the strong than it takes from the weak, and has its use even when levelled against what is good and true. In its own way it is a test of truth, and may be fearlessly applied to it as jewellers use nitric acid to try gold. If it be uttered for gold and is not gold, let it perish; but if it be true, it will stand trial.

The best translation of the works of Lucian into English was that by Dr. Thomas Francklin, sometime Greek Professor in the University of Cambridge, which was published in two large quarto volumes in the year 1780, and reprinted in four volumes in 1781. Lucian had been translated before in successive volumes by Ferrand Spence and others, an edition, completed in 1711, for which Dryden had written the author's Life. Dr. Francklin, who produced also the best eighteenth century translation of Sophocles, joined to his translation of Lucian a little apparatus of introductions and notes by which the English reader is often assisted, and he has skilfully avoided the translation of indecencies which never were of any use, and being no longer sources of enjoyment, serve only to exclude good wit, with which, under different conditions of life, they were associated, from the welcome due to it in all our homes. There is a just and scholarly, as well as a meddlesome and feeble way of clearing an old writer from uncleannesses that cause him now to be a name only where he should be a power. Dr. Francklin has understood his work in that way better than Dr. Bowdler did. He does not Bowdlerise who uses pumice to a blot, but he who rubs the copy into holes wherever he can find an honest letter with a downstroke thicker than becomes a fine-nibbed pen. A trivial play of fancy in one of the pieces in this volume, easily removed, would have been as a dead fly in the pot of ointment, and would have deprived one of Lucian's best works of the currency to which it is entitled.

Lucian's works are numerous, and they have been translated into nearly all the languages of Europe.

The "Instructions for Writing History" was probably one of the earliest pieces written by him after Lucian had settled down at Samosata to the free use of his pen, and it has been usually regarded as his best critical work. With ridicule of the affectations of historians whose names and whose books have passed into oblivion, he joins sound doctrine upon sincerity of style. "Nothing is lasting that is feigned," said Ben Jonson; "it will have another face ere long." Long after Lucian's day an artificial dignity, accorded specially to work of the historian, bound him by its conventions to an artificial style. He used, as Johnson said of Dr. Robertson, "too big words and too many of them." But that was said by Johnson in his latter days, with admission of like fault in the convention to which he had once conformed: "If Robertson's style is bad, that is to say, too big words and too many of them, I am afraid he caught it of me." Lucian would have dealt as mercilessly with that later style as Archibald Campbell, ship's purser and son of an Edinburgh Professor, who used the form of one of Lucian's dialogues, "Lexiphanes," for an assault of ridicule upon pretentious sentence-making, and helped a little to get rid of it. Lucian laughed in his day at small imitators of the manner of Thucydides, as he would laugh now at the small imitators of the manner of Macaulay. He bade the historian first get sure facts, then tell them in due order, simply and without exaggeration or toil after fine writing; though he should aim not the less at an enduring grace given by Nature to the Art that does not stray from her, and simply speaks the highest truth it knows.

The endeavour of small Greek historians to add interest to their work by magnifying the exploits of their countrymen, and piling wonder upon wonder, Lucian first condemned in his "Instructions for Writing History," and then caricatured in his "True History," wherein is contained the account of a trip to the moon, a piece which must have been enjoyed by Rabelais, which suggested to Cyrano de Bergerac his Voyages to the Moon and to the Sun, and insensibly contributed, perhaps, directly or through Bergerac, to the conception of "Gulliver's Travels." I have added the Icaro-Menippus, because that Dialogue describes another trip to the moon, though its satire is more especially directed against the philosophers.

Menippus was born at Gadara in Coele-Syria, and from a slave he grew to be a Cynic philosopher, chiefly occupied with scornful jests on his neighbours, and a money-lender, who made large gains and killed himself when he was cheated of them all. He is said to have written thirteen pieces which are lost, but he has left his name in literature, preserved by important pieces that have taken the name of "Menippean Satire."

Lucian married in middle life, and had a son. He was about fifty years old when he went to Paphlagonia, and visited a false oracle to detect the tricks of an Alexander who made profit out of it, and who professed to have a daughter by the Moon. When the impostor offered Lucian his hand to kiss, Lucian bit his thumb; he also intervened to the destruction of a profitable marriage for the daughter of the Moon. Alexander lent Lucian a vessel of his own for the voyage onward, and gave instructions to the sailors that they were to find a convenient time and place for throwing their passenger into the sea; but when the convenient time had come the goodwill of the master of the vessel saved Lucian's life. He was landed, therefore, at Ægialos, where he found some ambassadors to Eupator, King of Bithynia, who took him onward upon his way.

It is believed that Lucian lived to be ninety, and it is assumed, since he wrote a burlesque drama on gout, that the cause of his death was not simply old age. Gout may have been the immediate cause of death. Lucian must have spent much time at Athens, and he held office at one time in his later years as Procurator of a part of Egypt.

The works of Lucian consist largely of dialogues, in which he battled against what he considered to be false opinions by bringing the satire of Aristophanes and the sarcasm of Menippus into disputations that sought chiefly to throw down false idols before setting up the true. He made many enemies by bold attacks upon the ancient faiths. His earlier "Dialogues of the Gods" only brought out their stories in a way that made them sound ridiculous. Afterwards he proceeded to direct attack on the belief in them. In one Dialogue Timocles a Stoic argues for belief in the old gods against Damis an Epicurean, and the gods, in order of dignity determined by the worth of the material out of which they are made, assemble to hear the argument. Damis confutes the Stoic, and laughs him into fury. Zeus is unhappy at all this, but Hermes consoles him with the reflection that although the Epicurean may speak for a few, the mass of Greeks, and all the barbarians, remain true to the ancient opinions. Suidas, who detested such teaching, wrote a Life of him, in which he said that Lucian was at last torn to pieces by dogs.

Dr. Francklin prefaced his edition with a Life, written by a friend in the form of a Dialogue of the Dead in the Elysian Fields between Lord Lyttelton—who had been, in his Dialogues of the Dead, an imitator of the Dialogues so called in Lucian—and Lucian himself. "By that shambling gait and length of carcase," says Lucian, "it must be Lord Lyttelton coming this way." "And by that arch look and sarcastic smile," says Lyttelton, "you are my old friend Lucian, whom I have not seen this many a day. Fontenelle and I have just now been talking of you, and the obligations we both had to our old master: I assure you that there was not a man in all antiquity for whom, whilst on earth, I had a greater regard than yourself." After Lucian has told Lyttelton something about his life, his lordship thanks Lucian for the little history, and says, "I wish with all my heart I could convey it to a friend of mine in the other world"— meaning Dr. Francklin—"to whom, at this juncture, it would be of particular service: I mean a bold adventurer who has lately undertaken to give a new and complete translation of all your works. It is a noble design, but an arduous one; I own I tremble for him." Lucian replies, "I heard of it the other day from Goldsmith, who knew the man. I think he may easily succeed in it better than any of his countrymen, who hitherto have made but miserable work with me; nor do I make a much better appearance in my French habit, though that I know has been admired. D'Ablancourt has made me say a great many things, some good, some bad, which I never thought of, and, upon the whole, what he has done is more a paraphrase than a translation." Then, says Lord Lyttelton, "All the attempts to represent you, at least in our language, which I have yet seen, have failed, and all from the same cause, by the translator's departing from the original, and substituting his own manners, phraseology, expression, wit, and humour instead of yours. Nothing, as it has been observed by one of our best critics, is so grave as true humour, and every line of Lucian is a proof of it; it never laughs itself, whilst it sets the table in a roar; a circumstance which these gentlemen seem all to have forgotten: instead of the set features and serious aspect which you always wear when most entertaining, they present us for ever with a broad grin, and if you have the least smile upon your countenance make you burst into a vulgar horse-laugh: they are generally, indeed, such bad painters, that the daubing would never be taken for you if they had not written 'Lucian' under the picture. I heartily wish the Doctor better luck." Upon which the Doctor's friend makes Lucian reply: "And there is some reason to hope it, for I hear he has taken pains about me, has studied my features well before he sat down to trace them on the canvas, and done it *con amore*: if he brings out a good resemblance, I shall excuse the want of grace and beauty in his piece. I assure you I am not without pleasing expectation; especially as my friend Sophocles, who, you know, sat to him some time ago, tells me, though he is no Praxiteles, he does not take a bad likeness. But I must be gone, for yonder come Swift and Rabelais, whom I have made a little party with this morning: so, my good lord, fare you well."

Lucian had another translator in 1820, who in no way superseded Dr. Francklin. The reader of this volume is reminded that the notes are Dr. Francklin's, and that any allusion in them to a current topic, has to be read as if this present year of grace were 1780.

H. M.

INSTRUCTIONS FOR WRITING HISTORY.

Lucian, in this letter to his friend Philo, after having, with infinite humour, exposed the absurdities of some contemporary historians, whose works, being consigned to oblivion, have never reached us, proceeds, in the latter part of it, to lay down most excellent rules and directions for writing history. My readers will find the one to the last degree pleasant and entertaining; and the other no less useful, sensible, and instructive. This is, indeed, one of Lucian's best pieces.

My Dear Philo,—In the reign of Lysimachus, {17} we are told that the people of Abdera were seized with a violent epidemical fever, which raged through the whole city, continuing for seven days, at the expiration of which a copious discharge of blood from the nostrils in some, and in others a profuse sweat, carried it off. It was attended, however, with a very ridiculous circumstance: every one of the persons affected by it being suddenly taken with a fit of tragedising, spouting iambics, and roaring out most furiously, particularly the *Andromeda* {18a} of Euripides, and the speech of Perseus, which they recited in most lamentable accents. The city swarmed with these pale seventh-day patients, who, with loud voices, were perpetually bawling out—

"O tyrant love, o'er gods and men supreme," etc.

And this they continued every day for a long time, till winter and the cold weather coming on put an end to their delirium. For this disorder they seem, in my opinion, indebted to Archelaus, a tragedian at that time in high estimation, who, in the middle of summer, at the very hottest season {18b} of the year, exhibited the *Andromeda*, which had such an effect on the spectators that several of them, as soon as they rose up from it, fell insensibly into the tragedising vein; the *Andromeda* naturally occurring to their memories, and Perseus, with his Medusa, still hovering round them.

Now if, as they say, one may compare great things with small, this Abderian disorder seems to have seized on many of our *literati* of the present age; not that it sets them on acting tragedies (for the folly would not be so great in repeating other people's verses, especially if they were good ones), but ever since the war was begun against the barbarians, the defeat in Armenia, {19a} and the victories consequent on it, not one is there amongst us who does not write a history; or rather, I may say, we are all Thucydideses, Herodotuses, and Xenophons. Well may they say war is the parent of all things, {19b} when one action can make so many historians. This puts me in mind of what happened at Sinope. {20a}

When the Corinthians heard that Philip was going to attack them, they were all alarmed, and fell to work, some brushing up their arms, others bringing stones to prop up their walls and defend their bulwarks, every one, in short, lending a hand. Diogenes observing this, and having nothing to do (for nobody employed him), tucked up his robe, and, with all his might, fell a rolling his tub which he lived in up and down the Cranium. {20b} "What are you about?" said one of his friends. "Rolling my tub," replied he, "that whilst everybody is busy around me, I may not be the only idle person in the kingdom." In like manner, I, my dear Philo, being very loath in this noisy age to make no noise at all, or to act the part of a mute in the comedy, think it highly proper that I should roll my tub also; not that I mean to write history myself, or be a narrator of facts; you need not fear me, I am not so rash, knowing the danger too well if I roll it amongst the stones, especially such a tub as mine, which is not over-strong, so that the least pebble I strike against would dash it in pieces. I will tell you, however, what my design is—how I mean to be present at the battle and yet keep out of the reach of danger. I intend to shelter myself from the waves and the smoke, {21} and the cares that writers are liable to, and only give them a little good advice and a few precepts; to have, in short, some little hand in the building, though I do not expect my name will be inscribed on it, as I shall but just touch the mortar with the tip of my finger.

There are many, I know, who think there is no necessity for instruction at all with regard to this business, any more than there is for walking, seeing, or eating, and that it is the easiest thing in the world for a man to write history if he can but say what comes uppermost. But you, my friend, are convinced that it is no such easy matter, nor should it be negligently and carelessly performed; but that, on the other hand, if there be anything in the whole circle of literature that requires more than ordinary care and attention, it is undoubtedly this. At least, if a man would wish, as Thucydides says, to labour for posterity. I very well know that I cannot attack so many without rendering myself obnoxious to some, especially those whose histories are already finished and made public; even if what I say should be approved by them, it would be madness to expect that they should retract anything or alter that which had been once established and, as it were, laid up in royal repositories. It may not be amiss, however, to give them these instructions, that in case of another war, the Getæ against the Gauls, or the Indians, perhaps, against the barbarians (for with regard to ourselves there is no danger, our enemies being all subdued), by applying these rules if they like them, they may know better how to write for the future. If they do not choose this, they may even go on by their old measure; the physician will not break his heart if all the people of Abdera follow their own inclination and continue to act the *Andromeda*. {23}

Criticism is twofold: that which teaches us what we are to choose, and that which teaches us what to avoid. We will begin with the last, and consider what those faults are which a writer of history should be free from; next, what it is that will lead him into the right path, how he should begin, what order and method he should observe, what he should pass over in silence, and what he should dwell upon, how things may be best illustrated and connected. Of these, and such as these, we will speak hereafter; in the meantime let us point out the faults which bad writers are most generally guilty of, the blunders which they commit in language, composition, and sentiment, with many other marks of ignorance, which it would be tedious to enumerate, and belong not to our present argument. The principal faults, as I observed to you, are in the language and composition.

You will find on examination, that history in general has a great many of this kind, which, if you listen to them all, you will be sufficiently convinced of; and for this purpose it may not be unseasonable to recollect some of them by way of example. And the first that I shall mention is that intolerable custom which most of them have of omitting facts, and dwelling for ever on the praises of their generals and commanders, extolling to the skies their own leaders, and degrading beyond measure those of their enemies, not knowing how much history differs from panegyric, that there is a great wall between them, or that, to use a musical phrase, they are a double octave {24a} distant from each other; the sole business of the panegyrist is, at all events and by every means, to extol and delight the object of his praise, and it little concerns him whether it be true or not. But history will not admit the least degree of falsehood any more than, as physicians say, the wind-pipe {24b} can receive into it any kind of food.

These men seem not to know that poetry has its particular rules and precepts; and that history is governed by others directly opposite. That with regard to the former, the licence is immoderate, and there is scarce any law but what the poet prescribes to himself. When he is full of the Deity, and possessed, as it were, by the Muses, if he has a mind to put winged horses {25a} to his chariot, and drive some through the waters, and others over the tops of unbending corn, there is no offence taken. Neither, if his Jupiter {25b} hangs the earth and sea at the end of a chain, are we afraid that it should break and destroy us all. If he wants to extol

Agamemnon, who shall forbid his bestowing on him the head and eyes of Jupiter, the breast of his brother Neptune, and the belt of Mars? The son of Atreus and Ærope must be a composition of all the gods; nor are Jupiter, Mars, and Neptune sufficient, perhaps, of themselves to give us an idea of his perfection. But if history admits any adulation of this kind, it becomes a sort of prosaic poetry, without its numbers or magnificence; a heap of monstrous stories, only more conspicuous by their incredibility. He is unpardonable, therefore, who cannot distinguish one from the other; but lays on history the paint of poetry, its flattery, fable, and hyperbole: it is just as ridiculous as it would be to clothe one of our robust wrestlers, who is as hard as an oak, in fine purple, or some such meretricious garb, and put paint {26} on his cheeks; how would such ornaments debase and degrade him! I do not mean by this, that in history we are not to praise sometimes, but it must be done at proper seasons, and in a proper degree, that it may not offend the readers of future ages; for future ages must be considered in this affair, as I shall endeavour to prove hereafter.

Those, I must here observe, are greatly mistaken who divide history into two parts, the useful and the agreeable; and in consequence of it, would introduce panegyric as always delectable and entertaining to the reader. But the division itself is false and delusive; for the great end and design of history is to be useful: a species of merit which can only arise from its truth. If the agreeable follows, so much the better, as there may be beauty in a wrestler. And yet Hercules would esteem the brave though ugly Nicostratus as much as the beautiful Alcæus. And thus history, when she adds pleasure to utility, may attract more admirers; though as long as she is possessed of that greatest of perfections, truth, she need not be anxious concerning beauty.

In history, nothing fabulous can be agreeable; and flattery is disgusting to all readers, except the very dregs of the people; good judges look with the eyes of Argus on every part, reject everything that is false and adulterated, and will admit nothing but what is true, clear, and well expressed. These are the men you are to have a regard to when you write, rather than the vulgar, though your flattery should delight them ever so much. If you stuff history with fulsome encomiums and idle tales, you will make her like Hercules in Lydia, as you may have seen him painted, waiting upon Omphale, who is dressed in the lion's skin, with his club in her hand; whilst he is represented clothed in yellow and purple, and spinning, and Omphale beating him with her slipper; a ridiculous spectacle, wherein everything manly and godlike is sunk and degraded to effeminacy.

The multitude perhaps, indeed, may admire such things; but the judicious few whose opinion you despise will always laugh at what is absurd, incongruous, and inconsistent. Everything has a beauty peculiar to itself; but if you put one instead of another, the most beautiful becomes ugly, because it is not in its proper place. I need not add, that praise is agreeable only to the person praised, and disgustful to everybody else, especially when it is lavishly bestowed; as is the practice of most writers, who are so extremely desirous of recommending themselves by flattery, and dwell so much upon it as to convince the reader it is mere adulation, which they have not art enough to conceal, but heap up together, naked, uncovered, and totally incredible, so that they seldom gain what they expected from it; for the person flattered, if he has anything noble or manly in him, only abhors and despises them for it as mean parasites. Aristobulus, after he had written an account of the single combat between Alexander and Porus, showed that monarch a particular part of it, wherein, the better to get into his good graces, he had inserted a great deal more than was true; when Alexander seized the book and threw it (for they happened at that time to be sailing on the Hydaspes) directly into the river: "Thus," said he, "ought you to have been served yourself for pretending to describe my battles, and killing half a dozen elephants for me with a single spear." This anger was worthy of Alexander, of him who could not bear the adulation of that architect {29} who promised to transform Mount Athos into a statue of him; but he looked upon the man from that time as a base flatterer, and never employed him afterwards.

What is there in this custom, therefore, that can be agreeable, unless to the proud and vain; to deformed men or ugly women, who insist on being painted handsome, and think they shall look better if the artist gives them a little more red and white! Such, for the most part, are the historians of our times, who sacrifice everything to the present moment and their own interest and advantage; who can only be despised as ignorant flatterers of the age they live in; and as men, who, at the same time, by their extravagant stories, make everything which they relate liable to suspicion. If notwithstanding any are still of opinion, that the agreeable should be admitted in history, let them join that which is pleasant with that which is true, by the beauties of style and diction, instead of foisting in, as is commonly done, what is nothing to the purpose.

I will now acquaint you with some things I lately picked up in Ionia and Achaia, from several historians, who gave accounts of this war. By the graces I beseech you to give me credit for what I am going to tell you, as I could swear to the truth of it, if it were polite to swear in a dissertation. One of these gentlemen begins by invoking the Muses, and entreats the goddesses to assist him in the performance. What an excellent setting out and how properly is this form of speech adapted to history! A little farther on, he compares our emperor to Achilles, and the Persian king to Thersites; not considering that his Achilles would have been a much greater man if he had killed Hector rather than Thersites; if the brave should fly, he who pursues must be braver. Then follows an encomium on himself, showing how worthy he is to recite such noble actions; and when he is got on a little, he extols his own country, Miletus, adding that in this he had acted better than Homer, who never tells us where he was born. He informs us, moreover, at the end of his preface, in the most plain and positive terms, that he shall take care to make the best he can of our own affairs, and, as far as lies in his power, to get the upper hand of our enemies the barbarians. After investigating the cause of the war, he begins thus: "That vilest of all wretches, Vologesus, entered upon the war for these reasons." Such is this historian's manner. Another, a close imitator of Thucydides, that he may set out as his master does, gives us an exordium that smells of the true Attic honey, and begins thus: "Creperius Calpurnianus, a citizen of Pompeia, hath written the history of the war between the Parthians and the Romans, showing how they fought with one another, commencing at the time when it first broke out." After this, need I inform you how he harangued in Armenia, by another Corcyræan orator? or how, to be revenged of the Nisibæans for not taking part with the Romans, he sent the plague amongst them, taking the whole from Thucydides, excepting the long walls of Athens. He had begun from Æthiopia, descended into Egypt, and passed over great part of the royal territory. Well it was that he stopped there. When I left him, he was burying the miserable Athenians at Nisibis; but as I knew what he was going to tell us, I took my leave of him.

Another thing very common with these historians is, by way of imitating Thucydides, to make use of his phrases, perhaps with a little alteration, to adopt his manner, in little modes and expressions, such as, "you must yourself acknowledge," "for the same reason," "a little more, and I had forgot," and the like. This same writer, when he has occasion to mention bridges, fosses, or any of the machines used in war, gives them Roman names; but how does it suit the dignity of history, or resemble Thucydides, to mix the Attic and Italian thus, as if it was ornamental and becoming?

Another of them gives us a plain simple journal of everything that was done, such as a common soldier might have written, or a sutler who followed the camp. This, however, was tolerable, because it pretended to nothing more; and might be useful by supplying materials for some better historian. I only blame him for his pompous introduction: "Callimorphus, physician to the sixth legion of spearmen, his history of the Parthian war." Then his books are all carefully numbered, and he entertains us with a most frigid preface, which he concludes with saying that "a physician must be the fittest of all men to write history, because Æsculapius was the son of Apollo, and Apollo is the leader of the Muses, and the great prince of literature."

Besides this, after setting out in delicate Ionic, he drops, I know not how, into the most vulgar style and expressions, used only by the very dregs of the people.

And here I must not pass over a certain wise man, whose name, however, I shall not mention; his work is lately published at Corinth, and is beyond everything one could have conceived. In the very first sentence of his preface he takes his readers to task, and convinces them by the most sagacious method of reasoning that "none but a wise man should ever attempt to write history." Then comes syllogism upon syllogism; every kind of argument is by turns made use of, to introduce the meanest and most fulsome adulation; and even this is brought in by syllogism and interrogation. What appeared to me the most intolerable and unbecoming the long beard of a philosopher, was his saying in the preface that our emperor was above all men most happy, whose actions even philosophers did not disdain to celebrate; surely this, if it ought to be said at all, should have been left for us to say rather than himself.

Neither must we here forget that historian who begins thus: "I come to speak of the Romans and Persians;" and a little after he says, "for the Persians ought to suffer;" and in another place, "there was one Osroes, whom the Greeks call Oxyrrhoes," with many things of this kind. This man is just such a one as him I mentioned before, only that one is like Thucydides, and the other the exact resemblance of Herodotus.

But there is yet another writer, renowned for eloquence, another Thucydides, or rather superior to him, who most elaborately describes every city, mountain, field, and river, and cries out with all his might, "May the great averter of evil turn it all on our enemies!" This is colder than Caspian snow, or Celtic ice. The emperor's shield takes up a whole book to describe. The Gorgon's {35} eyes are blue, and black, and white; the serpents twine about his hair, and his belt has all the colours of the rainbow. How many thousand lines does it cost him to describe Vologesus's breeches and his horse's bridle, and how Osroes' hair looked when he swam over the Tigris, what sort of a cave he fled into, and how it was shaded all over with ivy, and myrtle, and laurel, twined together. You plainly see how necessary this was to the history, and that we could not possibly have understood what was going forward without it.

From inability, and ignorance of everything useful, these men are driven to descriptions of countries and caverns, and when they come into a multiplicity of great and momentous affairs, are utterly at a loss. Like a servant enriched on a sudden by coming into his master's estate, who does not know how to put on his clothes, or to eat as he should do; but when fine birds, fat sows, and hares are placed before him, falls to and eats till he bursts, of salt meat and pottage. The writer I just now mentioned describes the strangest wounds, and the most extraordinary deaths you ever heard of; tells us of a man's being wounded in the great toe, and expiring immediately; and how on Priscus, the general, bawling out loud, seven-and-twenty of the enemy fell down dead upon the spot. He has told lies, moreover, about the number of the slain, in contradiction to the account given in by the leaders. He will have it that seventy thousand two hundred and thirty-six of the enemy died at Europus, and of the Romans only two, and nine wounded. Surely nobody in their senses can bear this.

Another thing should be mentioned here also, which is no little fault. From the affectation of Atticism, and a more than ordinary attention to purity of diction, he has taken the liberty to turn the Roman names into Greek, to call Saturninus, Κρονιος, Chronius; Fronto, Φροντις, Frontis; Titianus, Τιτανιος, Titanius, and others still more ridiculous. With regard to the death of Severian, he informs us that everybody else was mistaken when they imagined that he perished by the sword, for that the man starved himself to death, as he thought that the easiest way of dying; not knowing (which was the case) that he could only have fasted three days, whereas many have lived without food for seven; unless we are to suppose that Osroes stood waiting till Severian had starved himself completely, and for that reason he would not live out the whole week.

But in what class, my dear Philo, shall we rank those historians who are perpetually making use of poetical expressions, such as "the engine crushed, the wall thundered," and in another place, "Edessa resounded with the shock of arms, and all was noise and tumult around;" and again, "often the leader in his mind revolved how best he might approach the wall." At the same time amongst these were interspersed some of the meanest and most beggarly phrases, such as "the leader of the army epistolised his master," "the soldiers bought utensils," "they washed and waited on them," with many other things of the same kind, like a tragedian with a high cothurnus on one foot and a slipper on the other. You will meet with many of these writers, who will give you a fine heroic long preface, that makes you hope for something extraordinary to follow, when after all, the body of the history shall be idle, weak, and trifling, such as puts you in mind of a sporting Cupid, who covers his head with the mask of a Hercules or Titan. The reader immediately cries out, "The mountain {39} has brought forth!" Certainly it ought not to be so; everything should be alike and of the same colour; the body fitted to the head, not a golden helmet, with a ridiculous breast-plate made of stinking skins, shreds, and patches, a basket shield, and hog-skin boots; and yet numbers of them put the head of a Rhodian Colossus on the body of a dwarf, whilst others show you a body without a head, and step directly into the midst of things, bringing in Xenophon for their authority, who begins with "Darius and Parysatis had two sons;" so likewise have other ancient writers; not considering that the narration itself may sometimes supply the place of preface, or exordium, though it does not appear to the vulgar eye, as we shall show hereafter.

All this, however, with regard to style and composition, may be borne with, but when they misinform us about places, and make mistakes, not of a few leagues, but whole day's journeys, what shall we say to such historians? One of them, who never, we may suppose, so much as conversed with a Syrian, or picked up anything concerning them in the barbers' {40} shop, when he speaks of Europus, tells us, "it is situated in Mesopotamia, two days' journey from Euphrates, and was built by the Edessenes." Not content with this, the same noble writer has taken away my poor country, Samosata, and carried it off, tower, bulwarks, and all, to Mesopotamia, where he says it is shut up between two rivers, which at least run close to, if they do not wash the walls of it. After this, it would be to no purpose, my dear Philo, for me to assure you that I am not from Parthia, nor do I belong to Mesopotamia, of which this admirable historian has thought fit to make me an inhabitant.

What he tells us of Severian, and which he swears he heard from those who were eye-witnesses of it, is no doubt extremely probable; that he did not choose to drink poison, or to hang himself, but was resolved to find out some new and tragical way of dying; that accordingly, having some large cups of very fine glass, as soon as he had taken the resolution to finish himself, he broke one of them in pieces, and with a fragment of it cut his throat; he would not make use of sword or spear, that his death might be more noble and heroic.

To complete all, because Thucydides {41} made a funeral oration on the heroes who fell at the beginning of the Peloponnesian war, he also thought something should be said of Severian. These historians, you must know, will always have a little struggle with Thucydides, though he had nothing to do with the war in Armenia; our writer, therefore, after burying Severian most magnificently, places at his sepulchre one Afranius Silo, a centurion, the rival of Pericles, who spoke so fine a declamation upon him as, by heaven, made me laugh till I cried again, particularly when the orator seemed deeply afflicted, and with tears in his eyes, lamented the sumptuous entertainments and drinking bouts which he should no more partake of. To crown all with an imitation of Ajax, {42} the orator draws his sword, and, as it became the noble Afranius, before all the assembly, kills himself at the tomb. So Mars defend me! but he deserved to die much sooner for making such a declamation. When those, says he, who were present beheld this, they were filled with admiration, and beyond measure extolled Afranius. For my own part, I pitied him for the loss of the cakes and dishes which he so lamented, and only blamed him for not destroying the writer of the history before he made an end of himself.

Others there are who, from ignorance and want of skill, not knowing what should be mentioned, and what passed over in silence, entirely omit or slightly run through things of the greatest consequence, and most worthy of attention, whilst they most copiously describe and dwell upon trifles; which is just as absurd as it would be not to take notice of or admire the wonderful beauty of the Olympian Jupiter, {43} and at the same time to be lavish in our praises of the fine polish, workmanship, and proportion of the base and pedestal.

I remember one of these who despatches the battle at Europus in seven lines, and spends some hundreds in a long frigid narration, that is nothing to the purpose, showing how "a certain Moorish cavalier, wandering on the mountains in search of water, lit on some Syrian rustics, who helped him to a dinner; how they were afraid of him at first, but afterwards became intimately acquainted with him, and received him with hospitality; for one of them, it seems, had been in Mauritania, where his brother bore arms." Then follows a long tale, "how he hunted in Mauritania, and saw several elephants feeding together; how he had like to have been devoured by a lion; and how many fish he bought at Cæsarea." This admirable historian takes no notice of the battle, the attacks or defences, the truces, the guards on each side, or anything else; but stands from morning to night looking upon Malchion, the Syrian, who buys cheap fish at Cæsarea: if night had not come on, I suppose he would have supped there, as the chars {44} were ready. If these things had not been carefully recorded in the history we should have been sadly in the dark, and the Romans would have had an insufferable loss, if Mausacas, the thirsty Moor, could have found nothing to drink, or returned to the camp without his supper; not to mention here, what is still more ridiculous, as how "a piper came up to them out of the neighbouring village, and how they made presents to each other, Mausacas giving Malchion a spear, and Malchion presenting Mausacas with a buckle." Such are the principal occurrences in the history of the battle of Europus. One may truly say of such writers that they never saw the roses on the tree, but took care to gather the prickles that grew at the bottom of it.

Another of them, who had never set a foot out of Corinth, or seen Syria or Armenia, begins thus: "It is better to trust our eyes than our ears; I write, therefore, what I have seen, and not what I have heard;" he saw everything so extremely well that he tells us, "the Parthian dragons (which amongst them signifies no more than a great number, {45} for one dragon brings a thousand) are live serpents of a prodigious size, that breed in Persia, a little above Iberia; that these are lifted up on long poles, and spread terror to a great distance; and that when the battle begins, they let them loose on the enemy." Many of our soldiers, he tells us, were devoured by them, and a vast number pressed to death by being locked in their embraces: this he beheld himself from the top of a high tree, to which he had retired for safety. Well it was for us that he so prudently determined not to come nigh them; we might otherwise have lost this excellent writer, who with his own brave hand performed such feats in this battle; for he went through many dangers, and was wounded somewhere about Susa, I suppose, in his journey from Cranium to Lerna. All this he recited to the Corinthians, who very well knew that he had never so much as seen a view of this battle painted on a wall; neither did he know anything of arms, or military machines, the method of disposing troops, or even the proper names of them. {46}

Another famous writer has given an account of everything that passed, from beginning to end, in Armenia, Syria, Mesopotamia, upon the Tigris, and in Media, and all in less than five hundred lines; and when he had done this, tells us, he has written a history. The title, which is almost as long as the work, runs thus: "A narrative of everything done by the Romans in Armenia, Media, and Mesopotamia, by Antiochianus, who gained a prize in the sacred games of Apollo." I suppose, when he was a boy, he had conquered in a running match.

I have heard of another likewise, who wrote a history of what was to happen hereafter, {47} and describes the taking of Vologesus prisoner, the murder of Osroes, and how he was to be given to a lion; and above all, our own much-to-be-wished-for triumph, as things that must come to pass. Thus prophesying away, he soon got to the end of the story. He has built, moreover, a new city in Mesopotamia, most magnificently magnificent, and most beautifully beautiful, and is considering with himself whether he shall call it Victoria, from victory, or the City of Concord, or Peace, which of them, however, is not yet determined, and this fine city must remain without a name, filled as it is with nothing but this writer's folly and nonsense. He is now going about a long voyage, and to give us a description of what is to be done in India; and this is more than a promise, for the preface is already made, and the third legion, the Gauls, and a small part of the Mauritanian forces under Cassius, have already passed the river; what they will do afterwards, or how they will succeed against the elephants, it will be some time before our wonderful writer can be able to learn, either from Mazuris or the Oxydraci.

Thus do these foolish fellows trifle with us, neither knowing what is fit to be done, nor if they did, able to execute it, at the same time determined to say anything that comes into their ridiculous heads; affecting to be grand and pompous, even in their titles: of "the Parthian victories so many books;" Parthias, says another, like Atthis; another more elegantly calls his book the Parthonicica of Demetrius.

I could mention many more of equal merit with these, but shall now proceed to make my promise good, and give some instructions how to write better. I have not produced these examples merely to laugh at and ridicule these noble histories; but with the view of real advantages, that he who avoids their errors, may himself learn to write well—if it be true, as the logicians assert, that of two opposites, between which there is no medium, the one being taken away, the other must remain. {49}

Somebody, perhaps, will tell me that the field is now cleansed and weeded, that the briars and brambles are cut up, the rubbish cleared off, and the rough path made smooth; that I ought therefore to build something myself, to show that I not only can pull down the structures of others, but am able to raise up and invent a work truly great and excellent, which nobody could find fault with, nor Momus himself turn into ridicule.

I say, therefore, that he who would write history well must be possessed of these two principal qualifications, a fine understanding and a good style: one is the gift of nature, and cannot be taught; the other may be acquired by frequent exercise, perpetual labour and an emulation of the ancients. To make men sensible and sagacious, who were not born so, is more than I pretend to; to create and new-model things in this manner would be a glorious thing indeed; but one might as easily make gold out of lead, silver out of tin, a Titornus out of a Conon, or a Milo out of a

Leotrophides. {50}

What then is in the power of art or instruction to perform? not to create qualities and perfections already bestowed, but to teach the proper use of them; for as Iccus, Herodicus, Theon, {51} or any other famous wrestler, would not promise to make Antiochus a conqueror in the Olympic games, or equal to a Theagenes, or Polydamas; but only that where a man had natural abilities for this exercise he could, by his instruction, render him a greater proficient in it: far be it from me, also, to promise the invention of an art so difficult as this, nor do I say that I can make anybody an historian; but that I will point out to one of good understanding, and who has been in some measure used to writing, certain proper paths (if such they appear to him), which if any man shall tread in, he may with greater ease and despatch do what he ought to do, and attain the end which he is in pursuit of.

Neither can it be here asserted, be he ever so sensible or sagacious, that he doth not stand in need of assistance with regard to those things which he is ignorant of; otherwise he might play on the flute or any other instrument, who had never learned, and perform just as well; but without teaching, the hands will do nothing; whereas, if there be a master, we quickly learn, and are soon able to play by ourselves.

Give me a scholar, therefore, who is able to think and to write, to look with an eye of discernment into things, and to do business himself, if called upon, who hath both civil and military knowledge; one, moreover, who has been in camps, and has seen armies in the field and out of it; knows the use of arms, and machines, and warlike engines of every kind; can tell what the front, and what the horn is, how the ranks are to be disposed, how the horse is to be directed, and from whence to advance or to retreat; one, in short, who does not stay at home and trust to the reports of others: but, above all, let him be of a noble and liberal mind; let him neither fear nor hope for anything; otherwise he will only resemble those unjust judges who determine from partiality or prejudice, and give sentence for hire: but, whatever the man is, as such let him be described. The historian must not care for Philip, when he loses his eye by the arrow of Aster, {53a} at Olynthus, nor for Alexander, when he so cruelly killed Clytus at the banquet: Cleon must not terrify him, powerful as he was in the senate, and supreme at the tribunal, nor prevent his recording him as a furious and pernicious man; the whole city of Athens must not stop his relation of the Sicilian slaughter, the seizure of Demosthenes, {53b} the death of Nicias, their violent thirst, the water which they drank, and the death of so many of them whilst they were drinking it. He will imagine (which will certainly be the case) that no man in his senses will blame him for recording things exactly as they fell out. However some may have miscarried by imprudence, or others by ill fortune, he is only the relator, not the author of them. If they are beaten in a sea-fight, it is not he who sinks them; if they fly, it is not he who pursues them; all he can do is to wish well to, and offer up his vows for them; but by passing over or contradicting facts, he cannot alter or amend them. It would have been very easy indeed for Thucydides, with a stroke of his pen, to have thrown down the walls of Epipolis, sunk the vessel of Hermocrates, or made an end of the execrable Gylippus, who stopped up all the avenues with his walls and ditches; to have thrown the Syracusans on the Lautumiæ, and have let the Athenians go round Sicily and Italy, according to the early hopes of Alcibiades: but what is past and done Clotho cannot weave again, nor Atropos recall.

The only business of the historian is to relate things exactly as they are: this he can never do as long as he is afraid of Artaxerxes, whose physician {55a} he is; as long as he looks for the purple robe, the golden chain, or the Nisæan horse, {55b} as the reward of his labours; but Xenophon, that just writer, will not do this, nor Thucydides. The good historian, though he may have private enmity against any man, will esteem the public welfare of more consequence to him, and will prefer truth to resentment; and, on the other hand, be he ever so fond of any man, will not spare him when he is in the wrong; for this, as I before observed, is the most essential thing in history, to sacrifice to truth alone, and cast away all care for everything else. The great universal rule and standard is, to have regard not to those who read now, but to those who are to peruse our works hereafter.

To speak impartially, the historians of former times were too often guilty of flattery, and their works were little better than games and sports, the effects of art. Of Alexander, this memorable saying is recorded: "I should be glad," said he, "Onesicritus, after my death, to come to life again for a little time, only to hear what the people then living will say of me; for I am not surprised that they praise and caress me now, as every one hopes by baiting well to catch my favour." Though Homer wrote a great many fabulous things concerning Achilles, the world was induced to believe him, for this only reason, because they were written long after his death, and no cause could be assigned why he should tell lies about him.

The good historian, {56} then, must be thus described: he must be fearless, uncorrupted, free, the friend of truth and of liberty; one who, to use the words of the comic poet, calls a fig a fig, {57a} and a skiff a skiff, neither giving nor withholding from any, from favour or from enmity, not influenced by pity, by shame, or by remorse; a just judge, so far benevolent to all as never to give more than is due to any in his work; a stranger to all, of no country, bound only by his own laws, acknowledging no sovereign, never considering what this or that man may say of him, but relating faithfully everything as it happened.

This rule therefore Thucydides observed, distinguishing properly the faults and perfections of history: not unmindful of the great reputation which Herodotus had acquired, insomuch that his books were called by the names of the Muses. {57b} Thucydides tells us that he "wrote for posterity, and not for present delight; that he by no means approved of the fabulous, but was desirous of delivering down the truth alone to future ages." It is the useful, he adds, which must constitute the merit of history, that by the retrospection of what is past, when similar events occur, men may know how to act in present exigencies.

Such an historian would I wish to have under my care: with regard to language and expression, I would not have it rough and vehement, consisting of long periods, {58} or complex arguments; but soft, quiet, smooth, and peaceable. The reflections, short and frequent, the style clear and perspicuous; for as freedom and truth should be the principal perfections of the writer's mind, so, with regard to language, the great point is to make everything plain and intelligible, not to use remote and far-fetched phrases or expressions, at the same time avoiding such as are mean and vulgar: let it be, in short, what the lowest may understand; and, at the same time, the most learned cannot but approve. The whole may be adorned with figure and metaphor, provided they are not turgid or bombast, nor seem stiff and laboured, which, like meat too highly seasoned, always give disgust.

History may sometimes assume a poetical form, and rise into a magnificence of expression, when the subject demands it; and especially when it is describing armies, battles, and sea-fights. The Pierian spirit {59} is wanting then to swell the sails with a propitious breeze, and carry the lofty ship over the tops of the waves. In general, the diction should creep humbly on the ground, and only be raised as the grand and beautiful occurring shall require it; keeping, in the meantime, within proper bounds, and never soaring into enthusiasm; for then it is in danger of ranging beyond its limits, into poetic fury: we must then pull in the rein and act with caution, well knowing that it is the worst vice of a writer, as well as of a horse, to be wanton and unmanageable. The best way therefore is, whilst the mind of the historian is on horseback, for his style to walk on foot, and take hold of the rein, that it may not be left behind.

With regard to composition, the words should not be so blended and transposed as to appear harsh and uncouth; nor should you, as some do, subject them entirely to the rhythmus; {60} one is always faulty, and the other disagreeable to the reader.

Facts must not be carelessly put together, but with great labour and attention. If possible, let the historian be an eye-witness of everything he means to record; or, if that cannot be, rely on those only who are incorrupt, and who have no bias from passion or prejudice, to add or to diminish anything. And here much sagacity will be requisite to find out the real truth. When he has collected all or most of his materials, he will first make a kind of diary, a body whose members are not yet distinct; he will then bring it into order and beautify it, add the colouring of style and language, adopt his expression to the subject, and harmonise the several parts of it; then, like Homer's Jupiter, {61} who casts his eye sometimes on the Thracian, and sometimes on the Mysian forces, he beholds now the Roman, and now the Persian armies, now both, if they are engaged, and relates what passes in them. Whilst they are embattled, his eye is not fixed on any particular part, nor on any one leader, unless, perhaps, a Brasidas {62a} steps forth to scale the walls, or a Demosthenes to prevent him. To the generals he gives his first attention, listens to their commands, their counsels, and their determination; and, when they come to the engagement, he weighs in equal scale the actions of both, and closely attends the pursuer and the pursued, the conqueror and the conquered. All this must be done with temper and moderation, so as not to satiate or tire, not inartificially, not childishly, but with ease and grace. When these things are properly taken care of, he may turn aside to others, ever ready and prepared for the present event, keeping time, {62b} as it were, with every circumstance and event: flying from Armenia to Media, and from thence with clattering wings to Italy, or to Iberia, that not a moment may escape him.

The mind of the historian should resemble a looking-glass, shining clear and exactly true, representing everything as it really is, and nothing distorted, or of a different form or colour. He writes not to the masters of eloquence, but simply relates what is done. It is not his to consider what he shall say, but only how it is to be said. He may be compared to Phidias, Praxiteles, Alcamenus, or other eminent artists; for neither did they make the gold, the silver, the ivory, or any of the materials which they worked upon. These were supplied by the Elians, the Athenians, and Argives; their only business was to cut and polish the ivory, to spread the gold into various forms, and join them together; their art was properly to dispose what was put into their hands; and such is the work of the historians, to dispose and adorn the actions of men, and to make them known with clearness and precision: to represent what he hath heard, as if he had been himself an eye-witness of it. To perform this well, and gain the praise resulting from it, is the business of our historical Phidias.

When everything is thus prepared, he may begin if he pleases without preface or exordium, unless the subject particularly demands it; he may supply the place of one, by informing us what he intends to write upon, in the beginning of the work itself: if, however, he makes use of any preface, he need not divide it as our orators do, into three parts, but confine it to two, leaving out his address to the benevolence of his readers, and only soliciting their attention and complacency: their attention he may be assured of, if he can convince them that he is about to speak of things great, or necessary, or interesting, or useful; nor need he fear their want of complacency, if he clearly explains to them the causes of things, and gives them the heads of what he intends to treat of.

Such are the exordiums which our best historians have made use of. Herodotus tells us, "he wrote his history, lest in process of time the memory should be lost of those things which in themselves were great and wonderful, which showed forth the victories of Greece, and the slaughter of the barbarians;" and Thucydides sets out with saying, "he thought that war most worthy to be recorded, as greater than any which had before happened; and that, moreover, some of the greatest misfortunes had accompanied it." The exordium, in short, may be lengthened or contracted according to the subject matter, and the transition from thence to the narration easy and natural. The body of the history is only a long narrative, and as such it must go on with a soft and even motion, alike in every part, so that nothing should stand too forward, or retreat too far behind. Above all, the style should be clear and perspicuous, which can only arise, as I before observed, from a harmony in the composition: one thing perfected, the next which succeeds should be coherent with it; knit together, as it were, by one common chain, which must never be broken: they must not be so many separate and distinct narratives, but each so closely united to what follows, as to appear one continued series.

Brevity is always necessary, especially when you have a great deal to say, and this must be proportioned to the facts and circumstances which you have to relate. In general, you must slightly run through little things, and dwell longer on great ones. When you treat your friends, you give them boars, hares, and other dainties; you would not offer them beans, saperda,

{66a} or any other common food.

When you describe mountains, rivers, and bulwarks, avoid all pomp and ostentation, as if you meant to show your own eloquence; pass over these things as slightly as you can, and rather aim at being useful and intelligible. Observe how the great and sublime Homer acts on these occasions! as great a poet as he is, he says nothing about Tantalus, Ixion, Tityus, and the rest of them. But if Parthenius, Euphorion, or Callimachus, had treated this subject, what a number of verses they would have spent in rolling Ixion's wheel, and bringing the water up to the very lips of Tantalus! Mark, also, how quickly Thucydides, who is very sparing {66b} of his descriptions, breaks off when he gives an account of any military machine, explains the manner of a siege, even though it be ever so useful and necessary, or describes cities or the port of Syracuse. Even in his narrative of the plague which seems so long, if you consider the multiplicity of events, you will find he makes as much haste as possible, and omits many circumstances, though he was obliged to retain so many more.

When it is necessary to make any one speak, you must take care to let him say nothing but what is suitable to the person, and to what he speaks about, and let everything be clear and intelligible: here, indeed, you may be permitted to play the orator, and show the power of eloquence. With regard to praise, or dispraise, you cannot be too modest and circumspect; they should be strictly just and impartial, short and seasonable: your evidence otherwise will not be considered as legal, and you will incur the same censure as Theopompus {67} did, who finds fault with everybody from enmity and ill-nature; and dwells so perpetually on this, that he seems rather to be an accuser than an historian.

If anything occurs that is very extraordinary or incredible, you may mention without vouching for the truth of it, leaving everybody to judge for themselves concerning it: by taking no part yourself, you will remain safe.

Remember, above all, and throughout your work, again and again, I must repeat it, that you write not with a view to the present times only, that the age you live in may applaud and esteem you, but with an eye fixed on posterity; from future ages expect your reward, that men may say of you, "that man was full of honest freedom, never flattering or servile, but in all things the friend of truth." This commendation, the wise man will prefer to all the vain hopes of this life, which are but of short duration.

Recollect the story of the Cnidian architect, when he built the tower in Pharos, where the fire is kindled to prevent mariners from running on the dangerous rocks of Parætonia, that most noble and most beautiful of all works; he carved his own name on a part of the rock on the inside, then covered it over with mortar, and inscribed on it the name of the reigning sovereign: well knowing that, as it afterwards happened, in a short space of time these letters would drop off with the mortar, and discover under it this inscription: "Sostratus the Cnidian, son of Dexiphanes, to those gods who preserve the mariner." Thus had he regard not to the times he lived in, not to his own short existence, but to the present period, and to all future ages, even as long as his tower shall stand, and his art remain upon earth.

Thus also should history be written, rather anxious to gain the approbation of posterity by truth and merit, than to acquire present applause by adulation and falsehood.

Such are the rules which I would prescribe to the historian, and which will contribute to the perfection of his work, if he thinks proper to observe them; if not, at least, I have rolled my tub. {69}

THE TRUE HISTORY.

BOOK I.

Lucian's True History is, as the author himself acknowledges in the Preface to it, a collection of ingenious lies, calculated principally to amuse the reader, not without several allusions, as he informs us, to the works of ancient Poets, Historians, and Philosophers, as well as, most probably, the performances of contemporary writers, whose absurdities are either obliquely glanced at, or openly ridiculed and exposed. We cannot but lament that the humour of the greatest part of these allusions must be lost to us, the works themselves being long since buried in oblivion. Lucian's True History, therefore, like the Duke of Buckingham's Rehearsal, cannot be half so agreeable as when it was first written; there is, however, enough remaining to secure it from contempt. The vein of rich fancy, and wildness of a luxuriant imagination, which run through the whole, sufficiently point out the author as a man of uncommon genius and invention. The reader will easily perceive that Bergerac, Swift, and other writers have read this work of Lucian's, and are much indebted to him for it.

PREFACE.

As athletics of all kinds hold it necessary, not only to prepare the body by exercise and discipline, but sometimes to give it proper relaxation, which they esteem no less requisite, so do I think it highly necessary also for men of letters, after their severer studies, to relax a little, that they may return to them with the greater pleasure and alacrity; and for this purpose there is no better repose than that which arises from the reading of such books as not only by their humour and pleasantry may entertain them, but convey at the same time some useful instruction, both which, I flatter myself, the reader will meet with in the following history; for he will not only be pleased with the novelty of the plan, and the variety of lies, which I have told with an air of truth, but with the tacit allusions so frequently made, not, I trust, without some degree of humour, to our ancient poets, historians, and philosophers, who have told us some most miraculous and incredible stories, and which I should have pointed out to you, but that I thought they would be sufficiently visible on the perusal.

Ctesias the Cnidian, son of Ctesiochus, wrote an account of India and of things there, which he never saw himself, nor heard from anybody else. Iambulus also has acquainted us with many wonders which he met with in the great sea, and which everybody knew to be absolute falsehoods: the work, however, was not unentertaining. Besides these, many others have likewise presented us with their own travels and peregrinations, where they tell us of wondrous large beasts, savage men, and unheard-of ways of living. The great leader and master of all this rhodomontade is Homer's "Ulysses," who talks to Alcinous about the winds {75} pent up in bags, man-eaters, and one-eyed Cyclops, wild men, creatures with many heads, several of his companions turned into beasts by enchantment, and a thousand things of this kind, which he related to the ignorant and credulous Phæacians.

These, notwithstanding, I cannot think much to blame for their falsehoods, seeing that the custom has been sometimes authorised, even by the pretenders to philosophy: I only wonder that they should ever expect to be believed: being, however, myself incited, by a ridiculous vanity, with the desire of transmitting something to posterity, that I may not be the only man who doth not indulge himself in the liberty of fiction, as I could not relate anything true (for I know of nothing at present worthy to be recorded), I turned my thoughts towards falsehood, a species of it, however, much more excusable than that of others, as I shall at least say one thing true, when I tell you that I lie, and shall hope to escape the general censure, by acknowledging that I mean to speak not a word of truth throughout. Know ye, therefore, that I am going to write about what I never saw myself, nor experienced, nor so much as heard from anybody else, and, what is more, of such things as neither are, nor ever can be. I give my readers warning, therefore, not to believe me.

* * * *

Once upon a time, {77} then, I set sail from the Pillars of Hercules, and getting into the Western Ocean, set off with a favourable wind; the cause of my peregrination was no more than a certain impatience of mind and thirst after novelty, with a desire of knowing where the sea ended, and what kind of men inhabited the several shores of it; for this purpose I laid in a large stock of provisions, and as much water as I thought necessary, taking along with me fifty companions of the same mind as myself. I prepared withal, a number of arms, with a skilful pilot, whom we hired at a considerable expense, and made our ship (for it was a pinnace), as tight as we could in case of a long and dangerous voyage.

We sailed on with a prosperous gale for a day and a night, but being still in sight of land, did not make any great way; the next day, however, at sun-rising, the wind springing up, the waves ran high, it grew dark, and we could not unfurl a sail; we gave ourselves up to the winds and waves, and were tossed about in a storm, which raged with great fury for threescore and nineteen days, but on the eightieth the sun shone bright, and we saw not far from us an island, high and woody, with the sea round it quite calm and placid, for the storm was over: we landed, got out, and happy to escape from our troubles, laid ourselves down on the ground for some time, after which we arose, and choosing out thirty of our company to take care of the vessel, I remained on shore with the other twenty, in order to take a view of the interior part of the island.

About three stadia from the sea, as we passed through a wood, we found a pillar of brass, with a Greek inscription on it, the characters almost effaced; we could make out however these words, "thus far came Hercules and Bacchus:" near it were the marks of two footsteps on a rock, one of them measured about an acre, the other something less; the smaller one appeared to me to be that of Bacchus, the larger that of Hercules; we paid our adorations to the deities and proceeded. We had not got far before we met with a river, which seemed exactly to resemble wine, particularly that of Chios; {79} it was of a vast extent, and in many places navigable; this circumstance induced us to give more credit to the inscription on the pillar, when we perceived such visible marks of Bacchus's presence here.

As I had a mind to know whence this river sprung, I went back to the place from which it seemed to arise, but could not trace the spring; I found, however, several large vines full of grapes, at the root of every one the wine flowed in great abundance, and from them I suppose the river was collected. We saw a great quantity of fish in it which were extremely like wine, both in taste and colour, and after we had taken and eaten a good many of them we found ourselves intoxicated; and when we cut them up, observed that they were full of grape stones; it occurred to us afterwards that we should have mixed them with some water fish, as by themselves they tasted rather too strong of the wine.

We passed the river in a part of it which was fordable, and a little farther on met with a most wonderful species of vine, the bottoms of them that touched the earth were green and thick, and all the upper part most beautiful women, with the limbs perfect from the waist, only that from the tops of the fingers branches sprung out full of grapes, just as Daphne is represented as turned into a tree when Apollo laid hold on her; on the head, likewise, instead of hair they had leaves and tendrils; when we came up to them they addressed us, some in the Lydian tongue, some in the Indian, but most of them in Greek; they would not suffer us to taste their grapes, but when anybody attempted it, cried out as if they were hurt.

We left them and returned to our companions in the ship. We then took our casks, filled some of them with water, and some with wine from the river, slept one night on shore, and the next morning set sail, the wind being very moderate. About noon, the island being now out of sight, on a sudden a most violent whirlwind arose, and carried the ship above three thousand stadia, lifting it up above the water, from whence it did not let us down again into the seas but kept us suspended {81a} in mid air, in this manner we hung for seven days and nights, and on the eighth beheld a large tract of land, like an island, {81b} round, shining, and remarkably full of light; we got on shore, and found on examination that it was cultivated and full of inhabitants, though we could not then see any of them. As night came on other islands appeared, some large, others small, and of a fiery colour; there was also below these another land with seas, woods, mountains, and cities in it, and this we took to be our native country: as we were advancing forwards, we were seized on a sudden by the Hippogypi, {82a} for so it seems they were called by the inhabitants; these Hippogypi are men carried upon vultures, which they ride as we do horses. These vultures have each three heads, and are immensely large; you may judge of their size when I tell you that one of their feathers is bigger than the mast of a ship. The Hippogypi have orders, it seems, to fly round the kingdom, and if they find any stranger, to bring him to the king: they took us therefore, and carried us before him. As soon as he saw us, he guessed by our garb what we were. "You are Grecians," said he, "are you not?" We told him we were. "And how," added he, "got ye hither through the air?" We told him everything that had happened to us; and he, in return, related to us his own history, and informed us, that he also was a man, that his name was Endymion, {82b} that he had been taken away from our earth in his sleep, and brought to this place where he reigned as sovereign. That spot, {83a} he told us, which now looked like a moon to us, was the earth. He desired us withal not to make ourselves uneasy, for that we should soon have everything we wanted. "If I succeed," says he, "in the war which I am now engaged in against the inhabitants of the sun, you will be very happy here." We asked him then what enemies he had, and what the quarrel was about? "Phaëton," he replied, "who is king of the sun {83b} (for that is inhabited as well as the moon), has been at war with us for some time past. The foundation of it was this: I had formerly an intention of sending some of the poorest of my subjects to establish a colony in Lucifer, which was uninhabited: but Phaëton, out of envy, put a stop to it, by opposing me in the mid-way with his Hippomyrmices; {84} we were overcome and desisted, our forces at that time being unequal to theirs. I have now, however, resolved to renew the war and fix my colony; if you have a mind, you shall accompany us in the expedition; I will furnish you everyone with a royal vulture and other accoutrements; we shall set out to-morrow." "With all my heart," said I, "whenever you please." We stayed, however, and supped with him; and rising early the next day, proceeded with the army, when the spies gave us notice that the enemy was approaching. The army consisted of a hundred thousand, besides the scouts and engineers, together with the auxiliaries, amongst whom were eighty thousand Hippogypi, and twenty thousand who were mounted on the Lachanopteri; {85a} these are very large birds, whose feathers are of a kind of herb, and whose wings look like lettuces. Next to these stood the Cinchroboli, {85b} and the Schorodomachi. {85c} Our allies from the north were three thousand Psyllotoxotæ {85d} and five thousand Anemodromi; {85e} the former take their names from the fleas which they ride upon, every flea being as big as twelve elephants; the latter are foot-soldiers, and are carried about in the air without wings, in this manner: they have large gowns hanging down to their feet, these they tuck up and spread in a form of a sail, and the wind drives them about like so many boats: in the battle they generally wear targets. It was reported that seventy thousand Strathobalani {86a} from the stars over Cappadocia were to be there, together with five thousand Hippogerani; {86b} these I did not see, for they never came: I shall not attempt, therefore, to describe them; of these, however, most wonderful things were related.

Such were the forces of Endymion; their arms were all alike; their helmets were made of beans, for they have beans there of a prodigious size and strength, and their scaly breast-plates of lupines sewed together, for the skins of their lupines are like a horn, and impenetrable; their shields and swords the same as our own.

The army ranged themselves in this manner: the right wing was formed by the Hippogypi, with the king, and round him his chosen band to protect him, amongst which we were admitted; on the left were the Lachanopteri; the auxiliaries in the middle, the foot were in all about sixty thousand myriads. They have spiders, you must know, in this country, in infinite numbers, and of pretty large dimensions, each of them being as big as one of the islands of the Cyclades; these were ordered to cover the air from the moon quite to the morning star; this being immediately done, and the field of battle prepared, the infantry was drawn up under the command of Nycterion, the son of Eudianax.

The left wing of the enemy, which was commanded by Phaëton himself, consisted of the Hippomyrmices; these are large birds, and resemble our ants, except with regard to size, the largest of them covering two acres; these fight with their horns and were in number about fifty thousand. In the right wing were the Aeroconopes, {87a} about five thousand, all archers, and riding upon large gnats. To these succeeded the Aerocoraces, {87b} light infantry, but remarkably brave and useful warriors, for they threw out of slings exceeding large radishes, which whoever was struck by, died immediately, a most horrid stench exhaling from the wound; they are said, indeed, to dip their arrows in a poisonous kind of mallow. Behind these stood ten thousand Caulomycetes, {88a} heavy-armed soldiers, who fight hand to hand; so called because they use shields made of mushrooms, and spears of the stalks of asparagus. Near them were placed the Cynobalani, {88b} about five thousand, who were sent by the inhabitants of Sirius; these were men with dog's heads, and mounted upon winged acorns: some of their forces did not arrive in time; amongst whom there were to have been some slingers from the Milky-way, together with the Nephelocentauri; {88c} they indeed came when the first battle was over, and I wish {88d} they had never come at all: the slingers did not appear, which, they say, so enraged Phaëton that he set their city on fire.

Thus prepared, the enemy began the attack: the signal being given, and the asses braying on each side, for such are the trumpeters they make use of on these occasions, the left wing of the Heliots, unable to sustain the onset of our Hippogypi, soon gave way, and we pursued them with great slaughter: their right wing, however, overcame our left. The Aeroconopes falling upon us with astonishing force, and advancing even to our infantry, by their assistance we recovered; and they now began to retreat, when they found the left wing had been beaten. The defeat then becoming general, many of them were taken prisoners and many slain; the blood flowed in such abundance that the clouds were tinged with it and looked red, just as they appear to us at sunset; from thence it distilled through upon the earth. Some such thing, I suppose, happened formerly amongst the gods, which made Homer believe that Jove {89} rained blood at the death of Sarpedon.

When we returned from our pursuit of the enemy we set up two trophies; one, on account of the infantry engagement in the spider's web, and another in the clouds, for our battle in the air. Thus prosperously everything went on, when our spies informed us that the Nephelocentaurs, who should have been with Phaëton before the battle, were just arrived: they made, indeed, as they approached towards us, a most formidable appearance, being half winged horses and half men; the men from the waist upwards, about as big as the Rhodian Colossus, and the horses of the size of a common ship of burthen. I have not mentioned the number of them, which was really so great, that it would appear incredible: they were commanded by Sagittarius, {90a} from the Zodiac. As soon as they learned that their friends had been defeated they sent a message to Phaëton to call him back, whilst they put their forces into order of battle, and immediately fell upon the Selenites, {90b} who were unprepared to resist them, being all employed in the division of the spoil; they soon put them to flight, pursued the king quite to his own city, and slew the greatest part of his birds; they then tore down the trophies, ran over all the field woven by the spiders, and seized me and two of my companions. Phaëton at length coming up, they raised other trophies for themselves; as for us, we were carried that very day to the palace of the Sun, our hands bound behind us by a cord of the spider's web.

The conquerors determined not to besiege the city of the Moon, but when they returned home, resolved to build a wall between them and the Sun, that his rays might not shine upon it; this wall was double and made of thick clouds, so that the moon was always eclipsed, and in perpetual darkness. Endymion, sorely distressed at these calamities, sent an embassy, humbly beseeching them to pull down the wall, and not to leave him in utter darkness, promising to pay them tribute, to assist them with his forces, and never more to rebel; he sent hostages withal. Phaëton called two councils on the affair, at the first of which they were all inexorable, but at the second changed their opinion; a treaty at length was agreed to on these conditions:—

The Heliots {92} and their allies on one part, make the following agreement with the Selenites and their allies on the other:—"That the Heliots shall demolish the wall now erected between them, that they shall make no irruptions into the territories of the Moon; and restore the prisoners according to certain articles of ransom to be stipulated concerning them; that the Selenites shall permit all the other stars to enjoy their rights and privileges; that they shall never wage war with the Heliots, but assist them whenever they shall be invaded; that the king of the Selenites shall pay to the king of the Heliots an annual tribute of ten thousand casks of dew, for the insurance of which, he shall send ten thousand hostages; that they shall mutually send out a colony to the Morning-star, in which, whoever of either nation shall think proper, may become a member; that the treaty shall be inscribed on a column of amber, in the midst of the air, and on the borders of the two kingdoms. This treaty was sworn to on the part of the Heliots, by Pyronides, {93} and Therites, and Phlogius; and on the part of the Selenites, by Nyctor, and Menarus, and Polylampus."

Such was the peace made between them; the wall was immediately pulled down, and we were set at liberty. When we returned to the Moon, our companions met and embraced us, shedding tears of joy, as did Endymion also. He intreated us to remain there, or to go along with the new colony; this I could by no means be persuaded to, but begged he would let us down into the sea. As he found I could not be prevailed on to stay, after feasting us most nobly for seven days, he dismissed us.

I will now tell you every thing which I met with in the Moon that was new and extraordinary. Amongst them, when a man grows old he does not die, but dissolves into smoke and turns to air. They all eat the same food, which is frogs roasted on the ashes from a large fire; of these they have plenty which fly about in the air, they get together over the coals, snuff up the scent of them, and this serves them for victuals. Their drink is air squeezed into a cup, which produces a kind of dew.

He who is quite bald is esteemed a beauty amongst them, for they abominate long hair; whereas, in the comets, it is looked upon as a perfection at least; so we heard from some strangers who were speaking of them; they have, notwithstanding, small beards a little above the knee; no nails to their feet, and only one great toe. They have honey here which is extremely sharp, and when they exercise themselves, wash their bodies with milk; this, mixed with a little of their honey, makes excellent cheese. {94} Their oil is extracted from onions, is very rich, and smells like ointment. Their wines, which are in great abundance, yield water, and the grape stones are like hail; I imagine, indeed, that whenever the wind shakes their vines and bursts the grape, then comes down amongst us what we call hail. They make use of their belly, which they can open and shut as they please, as a kind of bag, or pouch, to put anything in they want; it has no liver or intestines, but is hairy and warm within, insomuch, that new-born children, when they are cold, frequently creep into it. The garments of the rich amongst them are made of glass, but very soft: the poor have woven brass, which they have here in great abundance, and by pouring a little water over it, so manage as to card it like wool. I am afraid to mention their eyes, lest, from the incredibility of the thing, you should not believe me. I must, however, inform you that they have eyes which they take in and out whenever they please: so that they can preserve them anywhere till occasion serves, and then make use of them; many who have lost their own, borrow from others; and there are several rich men who keep a stock of eyes by them. Their ears are made of the leaves of plane-trees, except of those who spring, as I observed to you, from acorns, these alone have wooden ones. I saw likewise another very extraordinary thing in the king's palace, which was a looking-glass that is placed in a well not very deep; whoever goes down into the well hears everything that is said upon earth, and if he looks into the glass, beholds all the cities and nations of the world as plain as if he was close to them. I myself saw several of my friends there, and my whole native country; whether they saw me also I will not pretend to affirm. He who does not believe these things, whenever he goes there will know that I have said nothing but what is true.

To return to our voyage. We took our leave of the king and his friends, got on board our ship, and set sail. Endymion made me a present of two glass robes, two brass ones, and a whole coat of armour made of lupines, all which I left in the whale's belly. {96} He likewise sent with us a thousand Hippogypi, who escorted us five hundred stadia.

We sailed by several places, and at length reached the new colony of the Morning-star, where we landed and took in water; from thence we steered into the Zodiac; leaving the Sun on our left, we passed close by his territory, and would have gone ashore, many of our companions being very desirous of it, but the wind would not permit us; we had a view, however, of that region, and perceived that it was green, fertile, and well-watered, and abounding in everything necessary and agreeable. The Nephelocentaurs, who are mercenaries in the service of Phaëton, saw us and flew aboard our ship, but, recollecting that we were included into the treaty, soon departed; the Hippogypi likewise took their leave of us.

All the next night and day we continued our course downwards, and towards evening came upon Lycnopolis: {97} this city lies between the Pleiades and the Hyades, and a little below the Zodiac: we landed, but saw no men, only a number of lamps running to and fro in the market-place and round the port: some little ones, the poor, I suppose, of the place; others the rich and great among them, very large, light, and splendid: every one had its habitation or candlestick to itself, and its own proper name, as men have. We heard them speak: they offered us no injury, but invited us in the most hospitable manner; we were afraid, notwithstanding: neither would any of us venture to take any food or sleep. The king's court is in the middle of the city; here he sits all night, calls every one by name, and if they do not appear, condemns them to death for deserting their post; their death is, to be put out; we stood by and heard several of them plead their excuses for non-attendance. Here I found my own lamp, talked to him, and asked him how things went on at home; he told me everything that had happened. We stayed there one night, and next day loosing our anchor, sailed off very near the clouds; where we saw, and greatly admired the city of Nephelo-coccygia, {98a} but the wind would not permit us to land. Coronus, the son of Cottiphion, is king there. I remember Aristophanes, {98b} the poet, speaks of him, a man of wisdom and veracity, the truth of whose writings nobody can call in question. About three days after this, we saw the ocean very plainly, but no land, except those regions which hang in the air, and which appeared to us all bright and fiery. The fourth day about noon, the wind subsiding, we got safe down into the sea. No sooner did we touch the water, but we were beyond measure rejoiced. We immediately gave every man his supper, as much as we could afford, and afterwards jumped into the sea and swam, for it was quite calm and serene.

It often happens, that prosperity is the forerunner of the greatest misfortunes. We had sailed but two days in the sea, when early in the morning of the third, at sun-rise, we beheld on a sudden several whales, and one amongst them, of a most enormous size, being not less than fifteen hundred stadia in length, he came up to us with his mouth wide open, disturbing the sea for a long way before him, the waves dashing round on every side; he whetted his teeth, which looked like so many long spears, and were white as ivory; we embraced and took leave of one another, expecting him every moment; he came near, and swallowed us up at once, ship and all; he did not, however, crush us with his teeth, for the vessel luckily slipped through one of the interstices; when we were got in, for some time it was dark, and we could see nothing; but the whale happening to gape, we beheld a large space big enough to hold a city with ten thousand men in it; in the middle were a great number of small fish, several animals cut in pieces, sails and anchors of ships, men's bones, and all kinds of merchandise; there was likewise a good quantity of land and hills, which seemed to have been formed of the mud which he had swallowed; there was also a wood, with all sorts of trees in it, herbs of every kind; everything, in short, seemed to vegetate; the extent of this might be about two hundred and forty stadia. We saw also several sea-birds, gulls, and kingfishers, making their nests in the branches. At our first arrival in these regions, we could not help shedding tears; in a little time, however, I roused my companions, and we repaired our vessel; after which, we sat down to supper on what the place afforded. Fish of all kinds we had here in plenty, and the remainder of the water which we brought with us from the Morning-star. When we got up the next day, as often as the whale gaped, we could see mountains and islands, sometimes only the sky, and plainly perceived by our motion that he travelled through the sea at a great rate, and seemed to visit every part of it. At length, when our abode become familiar to us, I took with me seven of my companions, and advanced into the wood in order to see everything I could possibly; we had not gone above five stadia, before we met with a temple dedicated to Neptune, as we learned by the inscription on it, and a little farther on, several sepulchres, monumental stones, and a fountain of clear water; we heard the barking of a dog, and seeing smoke at some distance from us, concluded there must be some habitation not far off; we got on as fast as we could, and saw an old man and a boy very busy in cultivating a little garden, and watering it from a fountain; we were both pleased and terrified at the sight, and they, as you may suppose, on their part not less affected, stood fixed in astonishment and could not speak: after some time, however, "Who are you?" said the old man; "and whence come ye? are you daemons of the sea, or unfortunate men, like ourselves? for such we are, born and bred on land, though now inhabitants of another element; swimming along with this great creature, who carries us about with him, not knowing what is to become of us, or whether we are alive or dead." To which I replied, "We, father, are men as you are, and but just arrived here, being swallowed up, together with our ship, but three days ago; we came this way to see what the wood produced, for it seemed large and full of trees; some good genius led us towards you, and we have the happiness to find we are not the only poor creatures shut up in this great monster; but give us an account of your adventures, let us know who you are, and how you came here." He would not however, tell us anything himself, or ask us any questions, till he had performed the rites of hospitality; he took us into his house, therefore, where he had got beds, and made everything very commodious; here he presented us with herbs, fruit, fish, and wine: and when we were satisfied, began to inquire into our history; when I acquainted him with everything that had happened to us; the storm we met with; our adventures in the island; our sailing through the air, the war, etc., from our first setting out, even to our descent into the whale's belly.

He expressed his astonishment at what had befallen us, and then told us his own story, which was as follows:—"Strangers," said he, "I am a Cyprian by birth, and left my country to merchandise with this youth, who is my son, and several servants. We sailed to Italy with goods of various kinds, some of which you may, perhaps, have seen in the mouth of the whale; we came as far as Sicily with a prosperous gale, when a violent tempest arose, and we were tossed about in the ocean for three days, where we were swallowed up, men, ship and all, by the whale, only we two remaining alive; after burying our companions we built a temple to Neptune, and here we have lived ever since, cultivating our little garden, raising herbs, and eating fish or fruit. The wood, as you see, is very large, and produces many vines, from which we have excellent wine; there is likewise a fountain, which perhaps you have observed, of fresh and very cold water. We make our bed of leaves, have fuel sufficient, and catch a great many birds and live fish. Getting out upon the gills of the whale, there we wash ourselves when we please. There is a salt lake, about twenty stadia round, which produces fish of all kinds, and where we row about in a little boat which we built on purpose. It is now seven-and-twenty years since we were swallowed up. Everything here, indeed, is very tolerable, except our neighbours, who are disagreeable, troublesome, savage, and unsociable." "And are there more," replied I, "besides ourselves in the whale?" "A great many," said he, "and those very unhospitable, and of a most horrible appearance: towards the tail, on the western parts of the wood, live the Tarichanes, {104a} a people with eel's eyes, and faces like crabs, bold, warlike, and that live upon raw flesh. On the other side, at the right hand wall, are the Tritonomendetes, {104b} in their upper parts men, and in the lower resembling weasels. On the left are the Carcinochires, {104c} and the Thynnocephali, {104d} who have entered into a league offensive and defensive with each other. The middle part is occupied by the Paguradæ, {105a} and the Psittopodes, {105b} a warlike nation, and remarkably swift-footed. The eastern parts, near the whale's mouth, being washed by the sea, are most of them uninhabited. I have some of these, however, on condition of paying an annual tribute to the Psittopodes of five hundred oysters. Such is the situation of this country; our difficulty is how to oppose so many people, and find sustenance for ourselves." "How many may there be?" said I. "More than a thousand," said he. "And what are their arms?" "Nothing," replied he, "but fish-bones." "Then," said I, "we had best go to war with them, for we have arms and they none; if we conquer them we shall live without fear for the future." This was immediately agreed upon, and, as soon as we returned to our ship, we began to prepare. The cause of the war was to be the non-payment of the tribute, which was just now becoming due: they sent to demand it; he returned a contemptuous answer to the messengers: the Psittopodes and Paguradæ were both highly enraged, and immediately fell upon Scintharus (for that was the old man's name), in a most violent manner.

We, expecting to be attacked, sent out a detachment of five-and-twenty men, with orders to lie concealed till the enemy was past, and then to rise upon them, which they did, and cut off their rear. We, in the meantime, being likewise five-and-twenty in number, with the old man and his son, waited their coming up, met, and engaged them with no little danger, till at length they fled, and we pursued them even into their trenches. Of the enemy there fell an hundred and twenty; we lost only one, our pilot, who was run through by the rib of a mullet. That day, and the night after it, we remained on the field of battle, and erected the dried backbone of a dolphin as a trophy. Next day some other forces, who had heard of the engagement, arrived, and made head against us; the Tarichanes; under the command of Pelamus, in the right wing, the Thynnocephali on the left, and the Carcinochires in the middle; the Tritonomendetes remained neutral, not choosing to assist either party: we came round upon all the rest by the temple of Neptune, and with a hideous cry, rushed upon them. As they were unarmed, we soon put them to flight, pursued them into the wood, and took possession of their territory. They sent ambassadors a little while after to take away their dead, and propose terms of peace; but we would hear of no treaty, and attacking them the next day, obtained a complete victory, and cut them all off, except the Tritonomendetes, who, informed of what had passed, ran away up to the whale's gills, and from thence threw themselves into the sea. The country being now cleared of all enemies, we rambled through it, and from that time remained without fear, used what exercise we pleased, went a-hunting, pruned our vines, gathered our fruit, and lived, in short, in every respect like men put together in a large prison, which there was no escaping from, but where they enjoy everything they can wish for in ease and freedom; such was our way of life for a year and eight months.

On the fifteenth day of the ninth month, about the second opening of the whale's mouth (for this he did once every hour, and by that we calculated our time), we were surprised by a sudden noise, like the clash of oars; being greatly alarmed, we crept up into the whale's mouth, where, standing between his teeth, we beheld one of the most astonishing spectacles that was ever seen; men of an immense size, each of them not less than half a stadium in length, sailing on islands like boats. I know what I am saying is incredible, I shall proceed, notwithstanding: these islands were long, but not very high, and about a hundred stadia in circumference; there were about eight-and-twenty of these men in each of them, besides the rowers on the sides, who rowed with large cypresses, with their branches and leaves on; in the stern stood a pilot raised on an eminence and guiding a brazen helm; on the forecastle were forty immense creatures resembling men, except in their hair, which was all a flame of fire, so that they had no occasion for helmets; these were armed, and fought most furiously; the wind rushing in upon the wood, which was in every one of them, swelled it like a sail and drove them on, according to the pilot's direction; and thus, like so many long ships, the islands, by the assistance of the oars, also moved with great velocity. At first we saw only two or three, but afterwards there appeared above six hundred of them, which immediately engaged; many were knocked to pieces by running against each other, and many sunk; others were wedged in close together and, not able to get asunder, fought desperately; those who were near the prows showed the greatest alacrity, boarding each other's ships, and making terrible havoc; none, however, were taken prisoners. For grappling-irons they made use of large sharks chained together, who laid hold of the wood and kept the island from moving: they threw oysters at one another, one of which would have filled a waggon, and sponges of an acre long. Æolocentaurus was admiral of one of the fleets, and Thalassopotes {109} of the other: they had quarrelled, it seems, about some booty; Thalassopotes, as it was reported, having driven away a large tribe of dolphins belonging to Æolocentaurus: this we picked up from their own discourse, when we heard them mention the names of their commanders. At length the forces of Æolocentaurus prevailed, and sunk about a hundred and fifty of the islands of the enemy, and taking three more with the men in them: the rest took to their oars and fled. The conquerors pursued them a little way, and in the evening returned to the wreck, seizing the remainder of the enemy's vessels, and getting back some of their own, for they had themselves lost no less than fourscore islands in the engagement. They erected a trophy for this victory, hanging one of the conquered islands on the head of the whale, which they fastened their hawsers to, and casting anchor close to him, for they had anchors immensely large and strong, spent the night there: in the morning, after they had returned thanks, and sacrificed on the back of the whale, they buried their dead, sung their Io Pæans, and sailed off. Such was the battle of the islands.

BOOK II.

From this time our abode in the whale growing rather tedious and disagreeable, not able to bear it any longer, I began to think within myself how we might make our escape. My first scheme was to undermine the right-hand wall and get out there; and accordingly we began to cut away, but after getting through about five stadia, and finding it was to no purpose, we left off digging, and determined to set fire to the wood, which we imagined would destroy the whale, and secure us a safe retreat. We began, therefore, by burning the parts near his tail; for seven days and nights he never felt the heat, but on the eighth we perceived he grew sick, for he opened his mouth very seldom, and when he did, shut it again immediately; on the tenth and the eleventh he declined visibly, and began to stink a little; on the twelfth it occurred to us, which we had never thought of before, that unless, whilst he was gaping, somebody could prop up his jaws, to prevent his closing them, we were in danger of being shut up in the carcase, and perishing there: we placed some large beams, therefore, in his mouth, got our ship ready, and took in water, and everything necessary: Scintharus was to be our pilot: the next day the whale died; we drew our vessel through the interstices of his teeth, and let her down from thence into the sea: then, getting on the whale's back, sacrificed to Neptune, near the spot where the trophy was erected. Here we stayed three days, it being a dead calm, and on the fourth set sail; we struck upon several bodies of the giants that had been slain in the seafight, and measured them with the greatest astonishment: for some days we had very mild and temperate weather, but the north-wind arising, it grew so extremely cold, that the whole sea was froze up, not on the surface only, but three or four hundred feet deep, so that we got out and walked on the ice. The frost being so intense that we could not bear it, we put in practice the following scheme, which Scintharus put us in the head of: we dug a cave in the ice, where we remained for thirty days, lighting a fire, and living upon the fish which we found in it; but, our provisions failing, we were obliged to loosen our ship which was stuck fast in, and hoisting a sail, slid along through the ice with an easy pleasant motion; on the fifth day from that time, it grew warm, the ice broke, and it was all water again.

After sailing about three hundred stadia, we fell in upon a little deserted island: here we took in water, for ours was almost gone, killed with our arrows two wild oxen, and departed. These oxen had horns, not on their heads, but, as Momus seemed to wish, under their eyes. A little beyond this, we got into a sea, not of water, but of milk; and upon it we saw an island full of vines; this whole island was one compact well-made cheese, as we afterwards experienced by many a good meal, which we made upon it, and is in length five-and-twenty stadia. The vines have grapes upon them, which yield not wine, but milk. In the middle of the island was a temple to the Nereid {113} Galatæa, as appeared by an inscription on it: as long as we stayed there, the land afforded us victuals to eat, and the vines supplied us with milk to drink. Tyro, {114a} the daughter of Salmoneus, we were told, was queen of it, Neptune having, after her death, conferred that dignity upon her.

We stopped five days on this island, and on the sixth set sail with a small breeze, which gently agitated the waves, and on the eighth, changed our milky sea for a green and briny one, where we saw a great number of men running backwards and forwards, resembling ourselves in every part, except the feet, which were all of cork, whence, I suppose, they are called Phellopodes. {114b} We were surprised to see them not sinking, but rising high above the waves, and making their way without the least fear or apprehension; they came up to, and addressed us in the Greek tongue, telling us they were going to Phello, their native country; they accompanied us a good way, and then taking their leave, wished us a good voyage. A little after we saw several islands, amongst which, to the left of us, stood Phello, to which these men were going, a city built in the middle of a large round cork; towards the right hand, and at a considerable distance, were many others, very large and high, on which we saw a prodigious large fire: fronting the prow of our ship, we had a view of one very broad and flat, and which seemed to be about five hundred stadia off; as we approached near to it, a sweet and odoriferous air came round us, such as Herodotus tells us blows from Arabia Felix; from the rose, the narcissus, the hyacinth, the lily, the violet, the myrtle, the laurel, and the vine. Refreshed with these delightful odours, and in hopes of being at last rewarded for our long sufferings, we came close up to the island; here we beheld several safe and spacious harbours, with clear transparent rivers rolling placidly into the sea; meadows, woods, and birds of all kinds, chanting melodiously on the shore; and, on the trees, the soft and sweet air fanning the branches on every side, which sent forth a soft, harmonious sound, like the playing on a flute; at the same time we heard a noise, not of riot or tumult, but a kind of joyful and convivial sound, as of some playing on the lute or harp, with others joining in the chorus, and applauding them.

We cast anchor and landed, leaving our ship in the harbour with Scintharus and two more of our companions. As we were walking through a meadow full of flowers, we met the guardians of the isle, who, immediately chaining us with manacles of roses, for these are their only fetters, conducted us to their king. From these we learned, on our journey, that this place was called the Island of the Blessed, {116a} and was governed by Rhadamanthus. We were carried before him, and he was sitting that day as judge to try some causes; ours was the fourth in order. The first was that of Ajax Telamonius, {116b} to determine whether he was to rank with the heroes or not. The accusation ran that he was mad, and had made an end of himself. Much was said on both sides. At length Rhadamanthus pronounced that he should be consigned to the care of Hippocrates, and go through a course of hellebore, after which he might be admitted to the Symposium. The second was a love affair, to decide whether Theseus or Menelaus should possess Helen in these regions; and the decree of Rhadamanthus was, that she should live with Menelaus, who had undergone so many difficulties and dangers for her; besides, that Theseus had other women, the Amazonian lady and the daughters of Minos. The third cause was a point of precedency between Alexander the son of Philip, and Hannibal the Carthaginian, which was given in favour of Alexander, who was placed on a throne next to the elder Cyrus, the Persian. Our cause came on the last. The king asked us how we dared to enter, alone as we were, into that sacred abode. We told him everything that had happened; he commanded us to retire, and consulted with the assessors concerning us. There were many in council with him, and amongst them Aristides, the just Athenian, and pursuant to his opinion it was determined that we should suffer the punishment of our bold curiosity after our deaths, but at present might remain in the island for a certain limited time, associate with the heroes, and then depart; this indulgence was not to exceed seven months.

At this instant our chains, if so they might be called, dropped off, and we were left at liberty to range over the city, and to partake of the feast of the blessed. The whole city was of gold, {118} and the walls of emerald; the seven gates were all made out of one trunk of the cinnamon-tree; the pavement, within the walls, of ivory; the temples of the gods were of beryl, and the great altars, on which they offered the hecatombs, all of one large amethyst. Round the city flowed a river of the most precious ointment, a hundred cubits in breadth, and deep enough to swim in; the baths are large houses of glass perfumed with cinnamon, and instead of water filled with warm dew. For clothes they wear spider's webs, very fine, and of a purple colour. They have no bodies, but only the appearance of them, insensible to the touch, and without flesh, yet they stand, taste, move, and speak. Their souls seem to be naked, and separated from them, with only the external similitude of a body, and unless you attempt to touch, you can scarce believe but they have one; they are a kind of upright shadows, {119} only not black. In this place nobody ever grows old: at whatever age they enter here, at that they always remain. They have no night nor bright day, but a perpetual twilight; one equal season reigns throughout the year; it is always spring with them, and no wind blows but Zephyrus. The whole region abounds in sweet flowers and shrubs of every kind; their vines bear twelve times in the year, yielding fruit every month, their apples, pomegranates, and the rest of our autumnal produce, thirteen times, bearing twice in the month of Minos. Instead of corn the fields bring forth loaves of ready-made bread, like mushrooms. There are three hundred and sixty-five fountains of water round the city, as many of honey, and five hundred rather smaller of sweet-scented oil, besides seven rivers of milk and eight of wine.

Their symposia are held in a place without the city, which they call the Elysian Field. This is a most beautiful meadow, skirted by a large and thick wood, affording an agreeable shade to the guests, who repose on couches of flowers; the winds attend upon and bring them everything necessary, except wine, which is otherwise provided, for there are large trees on every side made of the finest glass, the fruit of which are cups of various shapes and sizes. Whoever comes to the entertainment gathers one or more of these cups, which immediately, becomes full of wine, and so they drink of it, whilst the nightingales and other birds of song, with their bills peck the flowers out of the neighbouring fields, and drop them on their heads; thus are they crowned with perpetual garlands. Their manner of perfuming them is this. The clouds suck up the scented oils from the fountains and rivers, and the winds gently fanning them, distil it like soft dew on those who are assembled there. At supper they have music also, and singing, particularly the verses of Homer, who is himself generally at the feast, and sits next above Ulysses, with a chorus of youths and virgins. He is led in accompanied by Eunomus the Locrian, {121a} Arion of Lesbos, Anacreon, and Stesichorus, {121b} whom I saw there along with them, and who at length is reconciled to Helen. When they have finished their songs, another chorus begins of swans, {122a} swallows, and nightingales, and to these succeeds the sweet rustling of the zephyrs, that whistle through the woods and close the concert. What most contributes to their happiness is, that near the symposium are two fountains, the one of milk, the other of pleasure; from the first they drink at the beginning of the feast; there is nothing afterwards but joy and festivity.

I will now tell you what men of renown I met with there. And first there were all the demigods, and all the heroes that fought at Troy except Ajax the Locrian, {122b} who alone, it seems, was condemned to suffer for his crimes in the habitations of the wicked. Then there were of the barbarians both the Cyruses, Anacharsis the Scythian, Zamolxis of Thrace, {123a} and Numa the Italian; {123b} besides these I met with Lycurgus the Spartan, Phocion and Tellus of Athens, and all the wise men except Periander. {123c} I saw also Socrates, the son of Sophroniscus, prating with Nestor and Palamedes; near him were Hyacinthus of Sparta, Narcissus the Thespian, Hylas, and several other beauties: he seemed very fond of Hyacinthus. Some things were laid to his charge: it was even reported that Rhadamanthus was very angry with him, and threatened to turn him out of the island if he continued to play the fool, and would not leave off his irony and sarcasm. Of all the philosophers, Plato {123d} alone was not to be found there, but it seems he lived in a republic of his own building, and which was governed by laws framed by himself. Aristippus and Epicurus were in the highest esteem here as the most polite, benevolent, and convivial of men. Even Æsop the Phrygian was here, whom they made use of by way of buffoon. Diogenes of Sinope had so wonderfully changed his manners in this place, that he married Lais the harlot, danced and sang, got drunk, and played a thousand freaks. Not one Stoic did I see amongst them; they, it seems, were not yet got up to the top of the high hill {124a} of virtue; and as to Chrysippus, we were told that he was not to enter the island till he had taken a fourth dose of hellebore. The Academicians, we heard, were very desirous of coming here, but they stood doubting and deliberating about it, neither were they quite certain whether there was such a place as Elysium or not; perhaps they were afraid of Rhadamanthus's judgment {124b} on them, as decisive judgments are what they would never allow. Many of them, it is reported, followed those who were coming to the island, but being too lazy to proceed, turned back when they were got half way.

Such were the principal persons whom I met with here. Achilles is had in the greatest honour among them, and next to him Theseus.

Two or three days after my arrival I met with the poet Homer, and both of us being quite at leisure, asked him several questions, and amongst the rest where he was born, that, as I informed him, having been long a matter of dispute amongst us. We were very ignorant indeed, he said, for some had made him a Chian, others a native of Smyrna, others of Colophon, but that after all he was a Babylonian, and amongst them was called Tigranes, though, after being a hostage in Greece, they had changed his name to Homer. I then asked him about those of his verses which are rejected as spurious, and whether they were his or not. He said they were all his own, which made me laugh at the nonsense of Zenodotus and Aristarchus the grammarians. I then asked him how he came to begin his "Iliad" with the wrath of Achilles; he said it was all by chance. I desired likewise to know whether, as it was generally reported, he wrote the "Odyssey" before the "Iliad." He said, no. It is commonly said he was blind, but I soon found he was not so; for he made use of his eyes and looked at me, so that I had no reason to ask him that question. Whenever I found him disengaged, I took the opportunity of conversing with him, and he very readily entered into discourse with me, especially after the victory which he obtained over Thersites, who had accused him of turning him into ridicule in some of his verses. The cause was heard before Rhadamanthus, and Homer came off victorious. Ulysses pleaded for him.

I met also Pythagoras the Samian, who arrived in these regions after his soul had gone a long round in the bodies of several animals, having been changed seven times. All his right side was of gold, and there was some dispute whether he should be called Pythagoras or Euphorbus. Empedocles came likewise, who looked sodden and roasted all over. He desired admittance, but though he begged hard for it, was rejected.

A little time after the games came on, which they call here Thanatusia. {126} Achilles presided for the fifth time, and Theseus for the seventh. A narrative of the whole would be tedious; I shall only, therefore, recount a few of the principal circumstances in the wrestling match. Carus, a descendant of Hercules, conquered Ulysses at the boxing match; Areus the Egyptian, who was buried at Corinth, and Epeus contended, but neither got the victory. The Pancratia was not proposed amongst them. In the race I do not remember who had the superiority. In poetry Homer was far beyond them all; Hesiod, however, got a prize. The reward to all was a garland of peacock's feathers.

When the games were over word was brought that the prisoners in Tartarus had broken loose, overcome the guard, and were proceeding to take possession of the island under the command of Phalaris the Agrigentine, {127a} Busiris of Egypt, {127b} Diomede the Thracian, {128a} Scyron, {128b} and Pityocamptes. As soon as Rhadamanthus heard of it he despatched the heroes to the shore, conducted by Theseus, Achilles, and Ajax Telamonius, who was now returned to his senses. A battle ensued, wherein the heroes were victorious, owing principally to the valour of Achilles. Socrates, who was placed in the right wing, behaved much better than he had done at Delius {128c} in his life-time, for when the enemy approached he never fled, nor so much as turned his face about. He had a very extraordinary present made him as the reward of his courage, no less than a fine spacious garden near the city; here he summoned his friends and disputed, calling the place by the name of the Academy of the Dead. They then bound the prisoners and sent them back to Tartarus, to suffer double punishment. Homer wrote an account of this battle, and gave it me to show it to our people when I went back, but I lost it afterwards, together with a great many other things. It began thus—

"Sing, Muse, the battles of the heroes dead—"

The campaign thus happily finished, they made an entertainment to celebrate the victory, which, as is usual amongst them, was a bean-feast. Pythagoras alone absented himself on that day, and fasted, holding in abomination the wicked custom of eating beans.

Six months had now elapsed, when a new and extraordinary affair happened. Cinyrus, the son of Scintharus, a tall, well-made, handsome youth, fell in love with Helen, and she no less desperately with him. They were often nodding and drinking to one another at the public feasts, and would frequently rise up and walk out together alone into the wood. The violence of his passion, joined to the impossibility of possessing her any other way, put Cinyrus on the resolution of running away with her. She imagined that they might easily get off to some of the adjacent islands, either to Phellus or Tyroessa. He selected three of the bravest of our crew to accompany them; never mentioning the design to his father, who he knew would never consent to it, but the first favourable opportunity, put it in execution; and one night when I was not with them (for it happened that I stayed late at the feast, and slept there) carried her off.

Menelaus, rising in the middle of the night, and perceiving that his wife was gone, made a dreadful noise about it, and, taking his brother along with him, proceeded immediately to the king's palace. At break of day the guards informed him that they had seen a vessel a good distance from land. He immediately put fifty heroes on board a ship made out of one large piece of the asphodelus, with orders to pursue them. They made all the sail they possibly could, and about noon came up with and seized on them, just as they were entering into the Milky Sea, close to Tyroessa; so near were they to making their escape. The pursuers threw a rosy chain over the vessel and brought her home again. Helen began to weep, blushed, and hid her face. Rhadamanthus asked Cinyrus and the rest of them if they had any more accomplices: they told him they had none. He then ordered them to be chained, whipped with mallows, and sent to Tartarus.

It was now determined that we should stay no longer on the island than the time limited, and the very next day was fixed for our departure. This gave me no little concern, and I wept to think I must leave so many good things, and be once more a wanderer. They endeavoured to administer consolation to me by assuring me that in a few years I should return to them again; they even pointed out the seat that should be allotted to me, and which was near the best and worthiest inhabitants of these delightful mansions. I addressed myself to Rhadamanthus, and humbly entreated him to inform me of my future fate, and let me know beforehand whether I should travel. He told me that, after many toils and dangers, I should at last return in safety to my native country, but would not point out the time when. He then showed me the neighbouring islands, five of which appeared near to me, and a sixth at a distance. "Those next to you," said he, "where you see a great fire burning, are the habitations of the wicked; the sixth is the city of dreams; behind that lies the island of Calypso, which you cannot see yet. When you get beyond these you will come to a large tract of land inhabited by those who live on the side of the earth directly opposite to you, {132} there you will suffer many things, wander through several nations, and meet with some very savage and unsociable people, and at length get into another region."

Having said thus, he took a root of mallow out of the earth, and putting it into my hand, bade me remember, when I was in any danger, to call upon that; and added, moreover, that if, when I came to the Antipodes, I took care "never to stir the fire with a sword, and never to eat lupines," I might have hopes of returning to the Island of the Blessed.

I then got everything ready for the voyage, supped with, and took my leave of them. Next day, meeting Homer, I begged him to make me a couple of verses for an inscription, which he did, and I fixed them on a little column of beryl, at the mouth of the harbour; the inscription was as follows:

"Dear to the gods, and favourite of heaven,
Here Lucian lived: to him alone 'twas given,
Well pleased these happy regions to explore,
And back returning, seek his native shore."

I stayed that day, and the next set sail; the heroes attending to take their leave of us; when Ulysses, unknown to Penelope, slipped a letter into my hand for Calypso, at the island of Ogygia. Rhadamanthus was so obliging as to send with us Nauplius the pilot, that, if we stopped at the neighbouring islands, and they should lay hold on us, he might acquaint them that we were only on our passage to another place.

As soon as we got out of the sweet-scented air, we came into another that smelt of asphaltus, pitch, and sulphur burning together, with a most intolerable stench, as of burned carcases: the whole element above us was dark and dismal, distilling a kind of pitchy dew upon our heads; we heard the sound of stripes, and the yellings of men in torment.

We saw but one of these islands; that which we landed on I will give you some description of. Every part of it was steep and filthy, abounding in rocks and rough mountains. We crept along, over precipices full of thorns and briers, and, passing through a most horrid country, came to the dungeon, and place of punishment, which we beheld with an admiration full of horror: the ground was strewed with swords and prongs, and close to us were three rivers, one of mire, another of blood, and another of fire, immense and impassable, that flowed in torrents, and rolled like waves in the sea; it had many fish in it, some like torches, others resembling live coals; which they called lychnisci. There is but one entrance into the three rivers, and at the mouth of them stood, as porter, Timon of Athens. By the assistance, however, of our guide, Nauplius, we proceeded, and saw several punished, {135a} as well kings as private persons, and amongst these some of our old acquaintance; we saw Cinyrus, {135b} hung up and roasting there. Our guides gave us the history of several of them, and told us what they were punished for; those, we observed, suffered most severely who in their lifetimes had told lies, or written what was not true, amongst whom were Ctesias the Cnidian, Herodotus, and many others. When I saw these I began to conceive good hopes of hereafter, as I am not conscious of ever having told a story.

Not able to bear any longer such melancholy spectacles, we took our leave of Nauplius, and returned to our ship. In a short time after we had a view, but confused and indistinct, of the Island of Dreams, which itself was not unlike a dream, for as we approached towards it, it seemed as it were to retire and fly from us. At last, however, we got up to it, and entered the harbour, which is called Hypnus, {136a} near the ivory gates, where there is a harbour dedicated to the cock. {136b} We landed late in the evening, and saw several dreams of various kinds. I propose, however, at present, to give you an account of the place itself, which nobody has ever written about, except Homer, whose description is very imperfect.

Round the island is a very thick wood; the trees are all tall poppies, or mandragoræ, {136c} in which are a great number of bats; for these are the only birds they have here; there is likewise a river which they call Nyctiporus, {136d} and round the gates two fountains: the name of one is Negretos, {137a} and of the other Pannychia. {137b} The city has a high wall, of all the colours of the rainbow. It has not two gates, as Homer {137c} tells us, but four; two of which look upon the plain of Indolence, one made of iron, the other of brick; through these are said to pass all the dreams that are frightful, bloody, and melancholy; the other two, fronting the sea and harbour, one of horn, the other, which we came through, of ivory; on the right hand, as you enter the city, is the temple of Night, who, together with the cock, is the principal object of worship amongst them. This is near the harbour; on the left is the palace of Somnus, for he is their sovereign, and under him are two viceroys, Taraxion, {138a} the son of Mataeogenes, and Plutocles, {138b} the son of Phantasion. In the middle of the market-place stands a fountain, which they call Careotis, {138c} and two temples of Truth and Falsehood; there is an oracle here, at which Antiphon presides as high-priest; he is inventor of the dreams, an honourable employment, which Somnus bestowed upon him.

The dreams themselves are of different kinds, some long, beautiful, and pleasant, others little and ugly; there are likewise some golden ones, others poor and mean; some winged and of an immense size, others tricked out as it were for pomps and ceremonies, for gods and kings; some we met with that we had seen at home; these came up to and saluted us as their old acquaintance, whilst others putting us first to sleep, treated us most magnificently, and promised that they would make us kings and noblemen: some carried us into our own country, showed us our friends and relations, and brought us back again the same day. Thirty days and nights we remained in this place, being most luxuriously feasted, and fast asleep all the time, when we were suddenly awaked by a violent clap of thunder, and immediately ran to our ship, put in our stores, and set sail. In three days we reached the island of Ogygia. Before we landed, I broke open the letter, and read the contents, which were as follows:

ULYSSES TO CALYPSO.

"This comes to inform you, that after my departure from your coasts in the vessel which you were so kind as to provide me with, I was shipwrecked, and saved with the greatest difficulty by Leucothea, who conveyed me to the country of the Phæacians, and from thence I got home; where I found a number of suitors about my wife, revelling there at my expense. I destroyed every one of them, and was afterwards slain myself by Telegonus, a son whom I had by Circe. I still lament the pleasures which I left behind at Ogygia, and the immortality which you promised me; if I can ever find an opportunity, I will certainly make my escape from hence, and come to you."

This was the whole of the epistle except, that at the end of it he recommended us to her protection.

On our landing, at a little distance from the sea, I found the cave, as described by Homer, and in it Calypso, spinning; she took the letter, put it in her bosom, and wept; then invited us to sit down, and treated us magnificently. She then asked us several questions about Ulysses, and inquired whether Penelope was handsome and as chaste as Ulysses had reported her to be. We answered her in such a manner as we thought would please her best; and then returning to our ship, slept on board close to the shore.

In the morning, a brisk gale springing up, we set sail. For two days we were tossed about in a storm; the third drove us on the pirates of Colocynthos. These are a kind of savages from the neighbouring islands, who commit depredations on all that sail that way. They have large ships made out of gourds, six cubits long; when the fruit is dry, they hollow and work it into this shape, using reeds for masts, and making their sails out of the leaves of the plant. They joined the crews of two ships and attacked us, wounding many of us with cucumber seeds, which they threw instead of stones. After fighting some time without any material advantage on either side, about noon we saw just behind them some of the Caryonautæ, {141a} whom we found to be avowed enemies to the Colocynthites, {141b} who, on their coming up, immediately quitted us, and fell upon them. We hoisted our sail, and got off, leaving them to fight it out by themselves; the Caryonautæ were most probably the conquerors, as they were more in number, for they had five ships, which besides were stronger and better built than those of the enemy, being made of the shells of nuts cut in two, and hollowed, every half-nut being fifty paces long. As soon as we got out of their sight, we took care of our wounded men, and from that time were obliged to be always armed and prepared in case of sudden attack. We had too much reason to fear, for scarce was the sun set when we saw about twenty men from a desert island advancing towards us, each on the back of a large dolphin. These were pirates also: the dolphins carried them very safely, and seemed pleased with their burden, neighing like horses. When they came up, they stood at a little distance, and threw dried cuttle-fish and crabs'-eyes at us; but we, in return, attacking them with our darts and arrows, many of them were wounded; and, unable to stand it any longer, they retreated to the island.

In the middle of the night, the sea being quite calm, we unfortunately struck upon a halcyon's nest, of an immense size, being about sixty stadia in circumference; the halcyon was sitting upon it, and was herself not much less; as she flew off, she was very near oversetting our ship with the wind of her wings, and, as she went, made a most hideous groaning. As soon as it was day we took a view of the nest, which was like a great ship, and built of trees; in it were five hundred eggs, each of them longer than a hogshead of Chios. We could hear the young ones croaking within; so, with a hatchet we broke one of the eggs, and took the chicken out unfledged; it was bigger than twenty vultures put together.

When we were got about two hundred stadia from the nest, we met with some surprising prodigies. A cheniscus came, and sitting on the prow of our ship, clapped his wings and made a noise. Our pilot Scintharus had been bald for many years, when on a sudden his hair came again. But what was still more wonderful, the mast of our ship sprouted out, sent forth several branches, and bore fruit at the top of it, large figs, and grapes not quite ripe. We were greatly astonished, as you may suppose, and prayed most devoutly to the gods to avert the evil which was portended.

We had not gone above five hundred stadia farther before we saw an immensely large and thick wood of pines and cypresses; we took it for a tract of land, but it was all a deep sea, planted with trees that had no root, which stood, however, unmoved, upright, and, as it were, swimming in it. Approaching near to it, we began to consider what we could do best. There was no sailing between the trees, which were close together, nor did we know how to get back. I got upon one of the highest of them, to see how far they reached, and perceived that they continued for about fifty stadia or more, and beyond that it was all sea again; we resolved therefore to drag the ship up to the top boughs, which were very thick, and so convey it along, which, by fixing a great rope to it, with no little toil and difficulty, we performed; got it up, spread our sails, and were driven on by the wind. It put me in mind of that verse of Antimachus the poet, where he says—

"The ship sailed smoothly through the sylvan sea."

We at length got over the wood, and, letting our ship down in the same manner, fell into smooth clear water, till we came to a horrid precipice, hollow and deep, resembling the cavity made by an earthquake. We furled our sails, or should soon have been swallowed up in it. Stooping forward, and looking down, we beheld a gulf of at least a thousand stadia deep, a most dreadful and amazing sight, for the sea as it were was split in two. Looking towards our right hand, however, we saw a small bridge of water that joined the two seas, and flowed from one into the other; we got the ship in here, and with great labour rowed her over, which we never expected.

From thence we passed into a smooth and calm sea, wherein was a small island with a good landing place, and which was inhabited by the Bucephali: a savage race of men, with bulls' heads and horns, as they paint the minotaur. As soon as we got on shore we went in search of water and provision, for we had none left; water we found soon, but nothing else; we heard, indeed, a kind of lowing at a distance, and expected to find a herd of oxen, but, advancing a little farther, perceived that it came from the men. As soon as they saw us, they ran after and took two of our companions; the rest of us got back to the ship as fast as we could. We then got our arms, and, determined to revenge our friends, attacked them as they were dividing the flesh of our poor companions: they were soon thrown into confusion and totally routed; we slew about fifty of them, and took two prisoners, whom we returned with. All this time we could get no provision. Some were for putting the captives to death, but not approving of this, I kept them bound till the enemy should send ambassadors to redeem them, which they did; for we soon heard them lowing in a melancholy tone, and most humbly beseeching us to release their friends. The ransom agreed on was a quantity of cheeses, dried fish, and onions, together with four stags, each having three feet, two behind and one before. In consideration of this, we released the prisoners, stayed one day there, and set sail.

We soon observed the fish swimming and the birds flying round about us, with other signs of our being near the land; and in a very little time after saw some men in the sea, who made use of a very uncommon method of sailing, being themselves both ships and passengers. I will tell you how they did it; they laid themselves all along in the water, they fastened to their middle a sail, and holding the lower part of the rope in their hands, were carried along by the wind. Others we saw, sitting on large casks, driving two dolphins who were yoked together, and drew the carriage after them: these did not run away from, nor attempt to do us any injury; but rode round about us without fear, observing our vessel with great attention, and seeming greatly astonished at it.

It was now almost dark, when we came in sight of a small island inhabited by women, as we imagined, for such they appeared to us, being all young and handsome, with long garments reaching to their feet. The island was called Cabalusa, and the city Hydamardia. {147a} I stopped a little, for my mind misgave me, and looking round, saw several bones and skulls of men on the ground; to make a noise, call my companions together, and take up arms, I thought would be imprudent. I pulled out my mallow, {147b} therefore, and prayed most devoutly that I might escape the present evil; and a little time afterwards, as one of the strangers was helping us to something, I perceived, instead of a woman's foot, the hoof of an ass. Upon this I drew my sword, seized on and bound her, and insisted on her telling me the truth with regard to everything about them. She informed me, much against her will, that she and the rest of the inhabitants were women belonging to the sea, that they were called Onoscileas, {148} and that they lived upon travellers who came that way. "We make them drunk," said she, "and when they are asleep, make an end of them." As soon as she had told me this, I left her bound there, and getting upon the house, called out to my companions, brought them together, showed them the bones, and led them in to her; when on a sudden she dissolved away into water, and disappeared. I dipped my sword into it by way of experiment, and the water turned into blood.

We proceeded immediately to our vessel and departed. At break of day we had a view of that continent which we suppose lies directly opposite to our own. Here, after performing our religious rites, and putting up our prayers, we consulted together about what was to be done next. Some were of opinion that, after making a little descent on the coast, we should turn back again; others were for leaving the ship there, and marching up into the heart of the country, to explore the inhabitants. Whilst we were thus disputing a violent storm arose, and driving our ship towards the land, split it in pieces. We picked up our arms, and what little things we could lay hold on, and with difficulty swam ashore.

Such were the adventures which befell us during our voyage, at sea, in the islands, in the air, in the whale, amongst the heroes, in the land of dreams, and lastly, amongst the Bucephali, and the Onoscileæ. What we met with on the other side of the world, shall be related in the ensuing books. {149}

ICARO-MENIPPUS. A DIALOGUE.

This Dialogue, which is also called by the commentators Ὑπερνεφελος, *or, "Above the Clouds," has a great deal of easy wit and humour in it, without the least degree of stiffness or obscurity; it is equally severe on the gods and philosophers; and paints, in the warmest colours, the glaring absurdity of the whole pagan system.*

MENIPPUS AND A FRIEND.
MENIPPUS.
Three thousand stadia {153} from the earth to the moon, my first resting-place; from thence up to the sun about five hundred parasangas; and from the sun to the highest heaven, and the palace of Jupiter, as far as a swift eagle could fly in a day.
FRIEND.
What are you muttering to yourself, Menippus, talking about the stars, and pretending to measure distances? As I walk behind you, I hear of nothing but suns and moons, parasangas, stations, and I know not what.
MENIPPUS.
Marvel not, my friend, if I utter things aërial and sublime; for I am recounting the wonders of my late journey.
FRIEND.
What! tracing your road by the stars, as the Phœnicians {154} do!
MENIPPUS.
Not so, by Jove! I have been amongst the stars themselves.
FRIEND.
You must have had a long dream, indeed, to travel so many leagues in it.
MENIPPUS.
It is no dream, I assure you; I am just arrived from Jupiter.
FRIEND.
How say you? Menippus let down from heaven?
MENIPPUS.
Even so: this moment come from thence, where I have seen and heard things most strange and miraculous. If you doubt the truth of them, the happier shall I be to have seen what is past belief.
FRIEND.
How is it possible, most heavenly and divine Menippus, that a mere mortal, like me, should dispute the veracity of one who has been carried above the clouds: one, to speak in the language of Homer, of the inhabitants {155} of heaven? But inform me, I beseech you, which way

you got up, and how you procured so many ladders; for, by your appearance, I should not take you for another Phrygian boy, {156} to be carried up by an eagle, and made a cup-bearer of.

MENIPPUS.

You are an old scoffer, I know, and therefore I am not surprised that an account of things above the comprehensions of the vulgar should appear like a fable to you; but, let me tell you, I wanted no ladders, nor an eagle's beak, to transport me thither, for I had wings of my own.

FRIEND.

This was beyond Dædalus himself, to be metamorphosed thus into a hawk, or jay, and we know nothing of it.

MENIPPUS.

You are not far from the mark, my friend; for my wings were a kind of Dædalian contrivance.

FRIEND.

Thou art a bold rogue indeed, and meant no doubt, if you had chanced to fall into any part of the ocean, to have called it, as Icarus {157a} did, by your own name, and styled it the Menippean Sea.

MENIPPUS.

Not so; his wings were glued on with wax, and when the sun melted it, could not escape falling; but mine had no wax in them.

FRIEND.

Indeed! now shall I quickly know the truth of this affair.

MENIPPUS.

You shall: I took, you must know, a very large eagle {157b} and a vulture also, one of the strongest I could get, and cut off their wings; but, if you have leisure, I will tell you the whole expedition from beginning to end.

FRIEND.

Pray do, for I long to hear it: by Jove the Friendly, I entreat thee, keep me no longer in suspense, for I am hung by the ears.

MENIPPUS.

Listen, then, for I would by no means baulk an inquisitive friend, especially one who is nailed by the ears, as you are. Finding, on a close examination, that everything here below, such as riches, honours, empire, and dominion, were all ridiculous and absurd, of no real value or estimation, considering them, withal, as so many obstacles to the study of things more worthy of contemplation, I looked up towards nobler objects, and meditated on the great universe before me; doubts immediately arose concerning what philosophers call the world; nor could I discover how it came into existence, its creator, the beginning or the end of it. When I descended to its several parts, I was still more in the dark: I beheld the stars, scattered as it were by the hand of chance, over the heavens; I saw the sun, and wished to know what it was; above all, the nature of the Moon appeared to me most wonderful and extraordinary; the diversity of its forms pointed out some hidden cause which I could not account for; the lightning also, which pierces through everything, the impetuous thunder, the rain, hail, and snow, {159} all raised my admiration, and seemed inexplicable to human reason. In this situation of mind, the best thing I thought which I could possibly do was to consult the philosophers; they, I made no doubt, were acquainted with the truth, and could impart it to me. Selecting, therefore, the best of them, as well as I could judge from the paleness and severity of their countenances, and the length of their beards (for they seemed all to be high-speaking and heavenly-minded men), into the hands of these I entirely resigned myself, and partly by ready money, partly by the promise of more, when they had made me completely wise, I engaged them to teach me the perfect knowledge of the universe, and how to talk on sublime subjects; but so far were they from removing my ignorance, that they only threw me into greater doubt and uncertainty, by puzzling me with atoms, vacuums, beginnings, ends, ideas, forms, and so forth: and the worst of all was, that though none agreed with the rest in what they advanced, but were all of contrary opinions, yet did every one of them expect that I should implicitly embrace his tenets, and subscribe to his doctrine.

FRIEND.

It is astonishing that such wise men should disagree, and, with regard to the same things, should not all be of the same opinion.

MENIPPUS.

You will laugh, my friend, when I shall tell you of their pride and impudence in the relation of extraordinary events; to think that men, who creep upon this earth, and are not a whit wiser, or can see farther than ourselves, some of them old, blind, and lazy, should pretend to know the limits and extent of heaven, measure the sun's circuit, and walk above the moon; that they should tell us the size and form of the stars, as if they were just come down from them; that those who scarcely know how many furlongs it is from Athens to Megara, should inform you exactly how many cubits distance the sun is from the moon, should mark out the height of the air, and the depth of the sea, describe circles, from squares upon triangles, make spheres, and determine the length and breadth of heaven itself: is it not to the last degree impudent and audacious? When they talk of things thus obscure and unintelligible, not merely to offer their opinions as conjectures, but boldly to urge and insist upon them: to do everything but swear, that the sun {161} is a mass of liquid fire, that the moon is inhabited, that the stars drink water, and that the sun draws up the moisture from the sea, as with a well-rope, and distributes his draught over the whole creation? How little they agree upon any one thing, and what a variety of tenets they embrace, is but too evident; for first, with regard to the world, their opinions are totally different; some affirm that it hath neither beginning nor end; some, whom I cannot but admire, point out to us the manner of its construction, and the maker of it, a supreme deity, whom they worship as creator of the universe; but they have not told us whence he came, nor where he exists; neither, before the formation of this world, can we have any idea of time or place.

FRIEND.

These are, indeed, bold and presumptuous diviners.

MENIPPUS.

But what would you say, my dear friend, were you to hear them disputing, concerning ideal {162} and incorporeal substances, and talking about finite and infinite? for this is a principal matter of contention between them; some confining all things within certain limits, others prescribing none. Some assert that there are many worlds, {163a} and laugh at those who affirm there is but one; whilst another, {163b} no man of peace, gravely assures us that war is the original parent of all things. Need I mention to you their strange opinions concerning the deities? One says, that number {163c} is a god; others swear by dogs, {164} geese, and plane-trees. Some give the rule of everything to one god alone, and take away all power from the rest, a scarcity of deities which I could not well brook; others more liberal, increased the number of gods, and gave to each his separate province and employment, calling one the first, and allotting to others the second or third rank of divinity. Some held that gods were incorporeal, and without form; others supposed them to have bodies. It was by no means universally acknowledged that the gods took cognisance of human affairs; some there were who exempted them from all care and solicitude, as we exonerate our old men from business and trouble; bringing them in like so many mute attendants on the stage. There are some too, who go beyond all this, and deny that there are any gods at all, but assert that the world is left without any guide or master.

I could not tell how to refuse my assent to these high-sounding and long-bearded gentlemen, and yet could find no argument amongst them all, that had not been refuted by some or other of them; often was I on the point of giving credit to one, when, as Homer says,

"To other thoughts,
My heart inclined." {165a}

The only way, therefore, to put an end to all my doubts, was, I thought, to make a bird of myself, and fly up to heaven. This my own eager desires represented as probable, and the fable-writer Æsop {165b} confirmed it, who carries up, not only his eagles, but his beetles, and camels thither. To make wings for myself was impossible, but to fit those of a vulture and an eagle to my body, might, I imagined, answer the same purpose. I resolved, therefore, to try the experiment, and cut off the right wing of one, and the left of the other; bound them on with thongs, and at the extremities made loops for my hands; then, raising myself by degrees, just skimmed above the ground, like the geese. When, finding my project succeed, I made a bold push, got upon the Acropolis {166a} and from thence slid down to the theatre. Having got so far without danger or difficulty, I began to meditate greater things, and setting off from Parnethes or Hymettus {166b} flew to Geranea, {166c} and from thence to the top of the tower at Corinth; from thence over Pholoe {166d} and Erymanthus quite to Taygetus. And now, resolving to strike a bold stroke, as I was already become a high flyer, and perfect in my art, I no longer confined myself to chicken flights, but getting upon Olympus, and taking a little light provision with me, I made the best of my way directly towards heaven. The extreme height which I soared to brought on a giddiness at first, but this soon went off; and when I got as far the Moon, having left a number of clouds behind me, I found a weariness, particularly in my vulture wing. I halted, therefore, to rest myself a little, and looking down from thence upon the earth, like Homer's Jupiter, beheld the places—

"Where the brave Mycians prove their martial force,
And hardy Thracians tame the savage horse;
Then India, Persia, and all-conquering Greece." {167}

which gave me wonderful pleasure and satisfaction.

FRIEND.

Let me have an exact account of all your travels, I beseech you, omit not the least particular, but give me your observations upon everything; I expect to hear a great deal about the form and figure of the earth, and how it all appeared to you from such an eminence.

MENIPPUS.

And so you shall; ascend, therefore, in imagination with me to the Moon, and consider the situation and appearance of the earth from thence: suppose it to seem, as it did to me, much less than the moon, insomuch, that when I first looked down, I could not find the high mountains, and the great sea; and, if it had not been for the Rhodian Colossus, {168} and the tower of Pharos, should not have known where the earth stood. At length, however, by the reflection of the sunbeams, the ocean appeared, and showed me the land, when, keeping my eyes fixed upon it, I beheld clearly and distinctly everything that was doing upon earth, not only whole nations and cities, but all the inhabitants of them, whether waging war, cultivating their fields, trying causes, or anything else; their women, animals, everything, in short, was before me.

FRIEND.

Most improbable, all this, and contradictory; you told me but just before, that the earth was so little by its great distance, that you could scarce find it, and, if it had not been for the Colossus, it would not have appeared at all; and now, on a sudden, like another Lynceus, you can spy out men, trees, animals, nay, I suppose, even a flea's nest, if you chose it.

MENIPPUS.

I thank you for putting me in mind of what I had forgot to mention. When I beheld the earth, but could not distinguish the objects upon it, on account of the immense distance, I was horribly vexed at it, and ready to cry, when, on a sudden, Empedocles {169} the philosopher stood behind me, all over ashes, as black as a coal, and dreadfully scorched: when I saw him, I must own I was frightened, and took him for some demon of the moon; but he came up to me, and cried out, "Menippus, don't be afraid,

"I am no god, why call'st thou me divine?" {170}

I am Empedocles, the naturalist: after I had leaped into the furnace, a vapour from Ætna carried me up hither, and here I live in the moon and feed upon dew: I am come to free you from your present distress." "You are very kind," said I, "most noble Empedocles, and when I fly back to Greece, I shall not forget to pay my devotions to you in the tunnel of my chimney every new moon." "Think not," replied he, "that I do this for the sake of any reward I might expect for it; by Endymion, {171} that is not the case, but I was really grieved to see you so uneasy: and now, how shall we contrive to make you see clear?" "That, by Jove," said I, "I cannot guess, unless you can take off this mist from my eyes, for they are horribly dim at present." "You have brought the remedy along with you." "How so?" "Have you not got an eagle's wing?" "True, but what has that to do with an eye?" "An eagle, you know, is more sharp-sighted than any other creature, and the only one that can look against the sun: your true royal bird is known by never winking at the rays, be they ever so strong." "So I have heard, and I am sorry I did not, before I came up, take out my own eyes and put in the eagle's; thus imperfect, to be sure, I am not royally furnished, but a kind of bastard bird." "You may have one royal eye, for all that, if you please; it is only when you rise up to fly, holding the vulture's wing still, and moving the eagle's only; by which means, you will see clearly with one, though not at all with the other." "That will do, and is sufficient for me; I have often seen smiths, and other artists, look with one eye only, to make their work the truer." This conversation ended, Empedocles vanished into smoke, and I saw no more of him. I acted as he advised me, and no sooner moved my eagle's wing, than a great light came all around me, and I saw everything as clear as possible: looking down to earth, I beheld distinctly cities and men, and everything that passed amongst them; not only what they did openly, but whatever was going on at home, and in their own houses, where they thought to conceal it. I saw Lysimachus betrayed by his son; {172a} Antiochus intriguing with his mother-in-law; {172b} Alexander the Thessalian slain by his wife; and Attalus poisoned by his son: in another place I saw Arsaces killing his wife, and the eunuch Arbaces drawing his sword upon Arsaces; Spartim, the Mede, dragged by the heels from the banquet by his guards, and knocked on the head with a cup. In the palaces of Scythia and Thrace the same wickedness was going forward; and nothing could I see but murderers, adulterers, conspirators, false swearers, men in perpetual terrors, and betrayed by their dearest friends and acquaintance.

Such was the employment of kings and great men: in private houses there was something more ridiculous; there I saw Hermodorus the Epicurean forswearing himself for a thousand drachmas; Agathocles the Stoic quarrelling with his disciples about the salary for tuition; Clinias the orator stealing a phial out of the temple; not to mention a thousand others, who were undermining walls, litigating in the forum, extorting money, or lending it upon usury; a sight, upon the whole, of wonderful variety.

FRIEND.

It must have been very entertaining; let us have it all, I desire.

MENIPPUS.

I had much ado to see, to relate it to you is impossible; it was like Homer's shield, {173} on one side were feasting and nuptials, on the other haranguing and decrees; here a sacrifice, and there a burial; the Getæ at war, the Scythians travelling in their caravans, the Egyptians tilling their fields, the Phœnicians merchandising, the Cilicians robbing and plundering, the Spartans flogging their children, and the Athenians perpetually quarrelling and going to law with one another.

When all this was doing, at the same time, you may conceive what a strange medley this appeared to me; it was just as if a number of dancers, or rather singers, were met together, and every one was ordered to leave the chorus, and sing his own song, each striving to drown the other's voice, by bawling as loud as he could; you may imagine what kind of a concert this would make.

FRIEND.
Truly ridiculous and confused, no doubt.

MENIPPUS.
And yet such, my friend, are all the poor performers upon earth, and of such is composed the discordant music of human life; the voices not only dissonant and inharmonious, but the forms and habits all differing from each other, moving in various directions, and agreeing in nothing; till at length the great master {175a} of the choir drives everyone of them from the stage, and tells him he is no longer wanted there; then all are silent, and no longer disturb each other with their harsh and jarring discord. But in this wide and extensive theatre, full of various shapes and forms, everything was matter of laughter and ridicule. Above all, I could not help smiling at those who quarrel about the boundaries of their little territory, and fancy themselves great because they occupy a Sicyonian {175b} field, or possess that part of Marathon which borders on Oenoe, or are masters of a thousand acres in Acharnæ; when after all, to me, who looked from above, Greece was but four fingers in breadth, and Attica a very small portion of it indeed. I could not but think how little these rich men had to be proud of; he who was lord of the most extensive country owned a spot that appeared to me about as large as one of Epicurus's atoms. When I looked down upon Peloponnesus, and beheld Cynuria, {176a} I reflected with astonishment on the number of Argives and Lacedemonians who fell in one day, fighting for a piece of land no bigger than an Egyptian lentil; and when I saw a man brooding over his gold, and boasting that he had got four cups or eight rings, I laughed most heartily at him: whilst the whole Pangæus, {176b} with all its mines, seemed no larger than a grain of millet.

FRIEND.
A fine sight you must have had; but how did the cities and the men look?

MENIPPUS.
You have often seen a crowd of ants running to and fro in and out of their city, some turning up a bit of dung, others dragging a bean-shell, or running away with half a grain of wheat. I make no doubt but they have architects, demagogues, senators, musicians, and philosophers amongst them. Men, my friend, are exactly like these: if you approve not of the

comparison, recollect, if you please, the ancient Thessalian fables, and you will find that the Myrmidons, {177} a most warlike nation, sprung originally from pismires.

When I had thus seen and diverted myself with everything, I shook my wings and flew off,

"To join the sacred senate of the skies." {178a}

Scarce had I gone a furlong, when the Moon, in a soft female voice, cried out to me, "Menippus, will you carry something for me to Jupiter, so may your journey be prosperous?" "With all my heart," said I, "if it is nothing very heavy." "Only a message," replied she, "a small petition to him: my patience is absolutely worn out by the philosophers, who are perpetually disputing about me, who I am, of what size, how it happens that I am sometimes round and full, at others cut in half; some say I am inhabited, others that I am only a looking-glass hanging over the sea, and a hundred conjectures of this kind; even my light, {178b} they say, is none of my own, but stolen from the Sun; thus endeavouring to set me and my brother together by the ears, not content with abusing him, and calling him a hot stone, and a mass of fire. In the meantime, I am no stranger to what these men, who look so grave and sour all day, are doing o' nights; but I see and say nothing, not thinking it decent to lay open their vile and abominable lives to the public; for when I catch them thieving, or practising any of their nocturnal tricks, I wrap myself up in a cloud, that I may not expose to the world a parcel of old fellows, who, in spite of their long beards, and professions of virtue, are guilty of every vice, and yet they are always railing at and abusing me. I swear by night I have often resolved to move farther off to get out of reach of their busy tongues; and I beg you would tell Jupiter that I cannot possibly stay here any longer, unless he will destroy these naturalists, stop the mouths of the logicians, throw down the Portico, burn the Academy, and make an end of the inhabitants of Peripatus; so may I enjoy at last a little rest, which these fellows are perpetually disturbing." "It shall be done," said I, and away I set out for heaven, where

"No tracks of beasts or signs of men are found." {179}

In a little time the earth was invisible, and the moon appeared very small; and now, leaving the sun on my right hand, I flew amongst the stars, and on the third day reached my journey's end. At first I intended to fly in just as I was, thinking that, being half an eagle, I should not be discovered, as that bird was an old acquaintance of Jupiter's, but then it occurred to me that I might be found out by my vulture's wing, and laid hold on: deeming it, therefore, most prudent not to run the hazard, I went up, and knocked at the door: Mercury heard me, and asking my name, went off immediately, and carried it to his master; soon after I was let in, and, trembling and quaking with fear, found all the gods sitting together, and seemingly not a little alarmed at my appearance there, expecting probably that they should soon have a number of winged mortals travelling up to them in the same manner: when Jupiter, looking at me with a most severe and Titanic {180a} countenance, cried out,

"Say who thou art, and whence thy country, name Thy parents—" {180b}

At this I thought I should have died with fear; I stood motionless, and astonished at the awfulness and majesty of his voice; but recovering myself in a short time, I related to him everything from the beginning, how desirous I was of knowing sublime truths, how I went to the philosophers, and hearing them contradict one another, and driven to despair, thought on the scheme of making me wings, with all that had happened in my journey quite up to heaven. I then delivered the message to him from the Moon, at which, softening his contracted brow, he smiled at me, and cried, "What were Otus and Ephialtes {181} in comparison of Menippus, who has thus dared to fly up to heaven; but come, we now invite you to supper with us; to-morrow we will attend to your business, and dismiss you." At these words he rose up and went to that part of heaven where everything from below could be heard most distinctly; for this, it seems, was the time appointed to hear petitions. As we went along, he asked me several questions about earthly matters, such as, "How much corn is there at present in Greece? had you a hard winter last year? and did your cabbages want rain? is any of Phidias's {182} family alive now? what is the reason that the Athenians have left off sacrificing to me for so many years? do they think of building up the Olympian temple again? are the thieves taken that robbed the Dodonæan?" When I had answered all these, "Pray, Menippus," said he, "what does mankind really think of me?" "How should they think of you," said I, "but with the utmost veneration, that you are the great sovereign of the gods." "There you jest," said he, "I am sure; I know well enough how fond they are of novelty, though you will not own it. There was a time, indeed, when I was held in some estimation, when I was the great physician, when I was everything, in short—

"When streets, and lanes, and all was full of Jove." {183a}

Pisa {183b} and Dodona {183c} were distinguished above every place, and I could not see for the smoke of sacrifices; but, since Apollo has set up his oracle at Delphi, and Æsculapius practises physic at Pergamus; since temples have been erected to Bendis {183d} at Thrace, to Anubis in Egypt, and to Diana at Ephesus, everybody runs after them; with them they feast, to them they offer up their hecatombs, and think it honour enough for a worn-out god, as I am, if they sacrifice once in six years at Olympia; whilst my altars are as cold and neglected as Plato's laws, {184} or the syllogisms of Chrysippus."

With this and such-like chat we passed away the time, till we came to the place where the petitions were to be heard. Here we found several holes, with covers to them, and close to every one was placed a golden chair. Jupiter sat down in the first he came to, and lifting up the lid, listened to the prayers, which, as you may suppose, were of various kinds. I stooped down and heard several of them myself, such as, "O Jupiter, grant me a large empire!" "O Jupiter, may my leeks and onions flourish and increase!" "Grant Jupiter, that my father may die soon!" "Grant I may survive my wife!" "Grant I may not be discovered, whilst I lay wait for my brother!" "Grant that I may get my cause!" "Grant that I may be crowned at Olympia!" One sailor asked for a north wind, another for a south; the husbandman prayed for rain, and the fuller for sunshine. Jupiter heard them all, but did not promise everybody—

"—some the just request,
He heard propitious, and denied the rest." {185a}

Those prayers which he thought right and proper he let up through the hole, and blew the wicked and foolish ones back, that they might not rise to heaven. One petition, indeed, puzzled him a little; two men asking favours of him directly contrary to each other, at the same time, and promising the same sacrifice; he was at a loss which to oblige; he became immediately a perfect Academic, and like Pyrrho, {185b} was held in suspense between them. When he had done with the prayers, he sat down upon the next chair, over another hole, and listened to those who were swearing and making vows. When he had finished this business, and destroyed Hermodorus, the Epicurean, for perjury, he removed to the next seat, and gave audience to the auguries, oracles, and divinations; which having despatched, he proceeded to the hole that brought up the fume of the victims, together with the name of the sacrificer. Then he gave out his orders to the winds and storms: "Let there be rain to-day in Scythia, lightning in Africa, and snow in Greece; do you, Boreas, blow in Lydia, and whilst Notus lies still, let the north wind raise the waves of the Adriatic, and about a thousand measures of hail be sprinkled over Cappadocia."

When Jupiter had done all his business we repaired to the feast, for it was now supper-time, and Mercury bade me sit down by Pan, the Corybantes, Attis, and Sabazius, a kind of demi-gods who are admitted as visitors there. Ceres served us with bread, and Bacchus with wine; Hercules handed about the flesh, Venus scattered myrtles, and Neptune brought us fish; not to mention that I got slyly a little nectar and ambrosia, for my friend Ganymede, out of good-nature, if he saw Jove looking another way, would frequently throw me in a cup or two. The greater gods, as Homer tells us {187a} (who, I suppose, had seen them as well as myself,) never taste meat or wine, but feed upon ambrosia and get drunk with nectar, at the same time their greatest luxury is, instead of victuals, to suck in the fumes that rise from the victims, and the blood of the sacrifices that are offered up to them. Whilst we were at supper, Apollo played on the harp, Silenus danced a cordax, and the Muses repeated Hesiod's Theogony, and the first Ode of Pindar. When these recreations were over we all retired tolerably well soaked, {187b} to bed,

"Now pleasing rest had sealed each mortal eye,
And even immortal gods in slumber lie,
All but myself—" {187c}

I could not help thinking of a thousand things, and particularly how it came to pass that, during so long a time Apollo {188a} should never have got him a beard, and how there came to be night in heaven, though the sun is always present there and feasting with them. I slept a little, and early in the morning Jupiter ordered the crier to summon a council of the gods, and when they were all assembled, thus addressed himself to them.

"The stranger who came here yesterday, is the chief cause of my convening you this day. I have long wanted to talk with you concerning the philosophers, and the complaints now sent to us from the Moon make it immediately necessary to take the affair into consideration. There is lately sprung up a race of men, slothful, quarrelsome, vain-glorious, foolish, petulant, gluttonous, proud, abusive, in short what Homer calls,

"An idle burthen to the ground." {188b}

These, dividing themselves into sects, run through all the labyrinths of disputation, calling themselves Stoics, Academics, Epicureans, Peripatetics, and a hundred other names still more ridiculous; then wrapping themselves up in the sacred veil of virtue, they contract their brows and let down their beards, under a specious appearance hiding the most abandoned profligacy; like one of the players on the stage, if you strip him of his fine habits wrought with gold, all that remains behind is a ridiculous spectacle of a little contemptible fellow, hired to appear there for seven drachmas. And yet these men despise everybody, talk absurdly of the gods, and drawing in a number of credulous boys, roar to them in a tragical style about virtue, and enter into disputations that are endless and unprofitable. To their disciples they cry up fortitude and temperance, a contempt of riches and pleasures, and, when alone, indulge in riot and debauchery. The most intolerable of all is, that though they contribute nothing towards the good and welfare of the community, though they are

"Unknown alike in council and in field;" {189}

yet are they perpetually finding fault with, abusing, and reviling others, and he is counted the greatest amongst them who is most impudent, noisy, and malevolent; if one should say to one of these fellows who speak ill of everybody, 'What service are you of to the commonwealth?' he would reply, if he spoke fairly and honestly, 'To be a sailor or a soldier, or a husbandman, or a mechanic, I think beneath me; but I can make a noise and look dirty, wash myself in cold water, go barefoot all winter, and then, like Momus, find fault with everybody else; if any rich man sups luxuriously, I rail at, and abuse him; but if any of my friends or acquaintance fall sick, and want my assistance, I take no notice of them.'

"Such, my brother gods, are the cattle {190} which I complain of; and of all these the Epicureans are the worst, who assert that the gods take no care of human affairs, or look at all into them: it is high time, my brethren, that we should take this matter into consideration, for if once they can persuade the people to believe these things, you must all starve; for who will sacrifice to you, when they can get nothing by it? What the Moon accuses you of, you all heard yesterday from the stranger; consult, therefore, amongst yourselves, and determine what may best promote the happiness of mankind, and our own security." When Jupiter had thus spoken, the assembly rung with repeated cries, of "thunder, and lightning! burn, consume, destroy! down with them into the pit, to Tartarus, and the giants!" Jove, however, once more commanding silence, cried out, "It shall be done as you desire; they and their philosophy shall perish together: but at present, no punishments must be inflicted; for these four months to come, as you all know, it is a solemn feast, and I have declared a truce: next year, in the beginning of the spring, my lightning shall destroy them.

"As to Menippus, first cutting off his wings that he may not come here again, let Mercury carry him down to the earth."

Saying this, he broke up the assembly, and Mercury taking me up by my right ear, brought me down, and left me yesterday evening in the Ceramicus. And now, my friend, you have heard everything I had to tell you from heaven; I must take my leave, and carry this good news to the philosophers, who are walking in the Pœcile.

NOTES.

{17} One of Alexander's generals, to whose share, on the division of the empire, after that monarch's death, fell the kingdom of Thrace, in which was situated the city of Abdera.

{18a} A small fragment of this tragedy, which has in it the very line here quoted by Lucian, is yet extant in Barnes's edition of Euripides.

{18b} This story may afford no useless admonition to the managers of the Haymarket and other summer theatres, who, it is to be hoped, will not run the hazard of inflaming their audiences with too much tragedy in the dog days.

{19a} This alludes to the Parthian War, in the time of Severian; the particulars of which, except the few here occasionally glanced at, we are strangers to. Lucian, most probably, by this tract totally knocked up some of the historians who had given an account of it, and prevented many others, who were intimidated by the severity of his strictures, attempting to transmit the history of it to posterity.

{19b} This saying is attributed to Empedocles.

{20a} The most famous of the Pontic cities, and well known as the residence of the renowned Cynic philosopher. It is still called by the same name, and is a port town of Asiatic Turkey, on the Euxine.

{20b} A kind of school or gymnasium where the young men performed their exercises. The choice of such a place by a philosopher to roll a tub in heightens the ridicule.

{21} See Homer's "Odyssey," M 1. 219.

{23} Alluding to the story he set out with.

{24a} διοδιαπασων. Gr. The Latin translation renders it "*octava duplici.*" See Burney's "Dissertation on Music," Sect. 1.

{24b} Gr. Την αρτηριαν τραχειαν, *aspera arteria*, or the wind-pipe. The comparison is strictly just and remarkably true, as we may all recollect how dreadful the sensation is when any part of our food slips down what is generally called "the wrong way."

{25a} See Homer's "Iliad," Υ 1. 227, and Virgil's "Camilla," in the 7th book of the "Æneid."

{25b} See Homer's "Iliad," υ 1. 18. One of the blind bard's *speciosa miracula*, which Lucian is perpetually laughing at.

{26} ψιμμυδιον, or cerussa. Painting, we see, both amongst men and women, was practised long ago, and has at least the plea of antiquity in its favour. According to Lucian, the men laid on white; for the ψιμμυδιον was probably ceruse, or white lead; the ladies, we may suppose, as at present, preferred the rouge.

{29} Dinocrates. The same story is told of him, with some little alteration, by Vitruvius. Mention is made of it likewise by Pliny and Strabo.

{35} "His buckler's mighty orb was next displayed;
Tremendous Gorgon frowned upon its field,
And circling terrors filled the expressive shield.
Within its concave hung a silver thong,
On which a mimic serpent creeps along,
His azure length in easy waves extends,
Till, in three heads, th' embroidered monster ends."
See Pope's "Homer's Iliad," book xi., 1. 43.
Lucian here means to ridicule, not Homer, but the historian's absurd imitation of him.

{39} The Greek expression was proverbial. Horace has adopted it: "Parturiunt montes, nascetur ridiculus mus."

{40} Lucian adds, το λεγομενον, ut est in proverbio, by which it appears that barbers and their shops were as remarkable for gossiping and tittle-tattle in ancient as they are in modern times. Aristophanes mentions them in his "Plutus," they are recorded also by Plutarch, and Theophrastus styles them αοινα συμποσια.

{41} See Thucydides, book ii., cap. 34.

{42} Who fell upon his sword. See the "Ajax" of Sophocles.

{43} For a description of this famous statue, see Pausanias.

{44} The σκαρος, or scarus, is mentioned by several ancient authors, as a fish of the most delicate flavour, and is supposed to be of the same nature with our chars in Cumberland, and some other parts of this kingdom. I have ventured, therefore, to call it by this name, till some modern Apicius can furnish me with a better.

{45} Dragons, or fiery serpents, were used by the Parthians, and Suidas tells us, by the Scythians also, as standards, in the same manner as the Romans made use of the eagle, and under every one of these standards were a thousand men. See Lips. de Mil. Rom., cap. 4.

{46} See Arrian.

{47} The idea here so deservedly laughed at, of a history of what was to come, if treated, not seriously, as this absurd writer treated it, but ludicrously, as Lucian would probably have treated it himself, might open a fine field for wit and humour. Something of this kind appeared in a newspaper a few years ago, which, I think, was called "News for a

Hundred Years Hence;" and though but a rough sketch, was well executed. A larger work, on the same ground, and by a good hand, might afford much entertainment.

{49} This kind of scholastic jargon was much in vogue in the time of Lucian, and it is no wonder he should take every opportunity of laughing at it, as nothing can be more opposite to true genius, wit, and humour, than such pedantry.

{50} Milo, the Crotonian wrestler, is reported to have been a man of most wonderful bodily strength, concerning which a number of lies are told, for which the reader, if he pleases, may consult his dictionary. He lost his life, we are informed, by trying to rend with his hands an old oak, which wedged him in, and pressed him to death; the poet says—
"—he met his end,
Wedged in that timber which he strove to rend."
Titornus was a rival of Milo's, and, according to Ælian, who is not always to be credited, rolled a large stone with ease, which Milo with all his force could not stir. Conon was some slim Macaroni of that age, remarkable only for his debility, as was Leotrophides also, of crazy memory, recorded by Aristophanes, in his comedy called *The Birds*.

{51} The Broughtons of antiquity; men, we may suppose, renowned in their time for teaching the young nobility of Greece to bruise one another *secundum artem*.

{53a} See Diodorus Siculus, lib. vii., and Plutarch.

{53b} Concerning some of these facts, even recent as they were then with regard to us, historians are divided. Thucydides and Plutarch tell the story one way, Diodorus and Justin another. Well might our author, therefore, find fault with their uncertainty.

{55a} Lucian alludes, it is supposed, to Ctesias, the physician to Artaxerxes, whose history is stuffed with encomiums on his royal patron. See Plutarch's "Artaxerxes."

{55b} The Campus Nisæus, a large plain in Media, near the Caspian mountains, was famous for breeding the finest horses, which were allotted to the use of kings only; or, according to Xenophon, those favourites on whom the sovereign thought proper to bestow them. See the "Cyropæd.," book viii.

{56} This fine picture of a good historian has been copied by Tully, Strabo, Polybius, and other writers; it is a standard of perfection, however, which few writers, ancient or modern, have been able to reach. Thuanus has prefixed to his history these lines of Lucian; but whether he, or any other historian, hath answered in every point to the description here given, is, I believe, yet undetermined.

{57a} The saying is attributed to Aristophanes, though I cannot find it there. It is observable that this proverbial kind of expression, for freedom of words and sentiments, has been adopted into almost every language, though the image conveying it is different. Thus the Greeks call a fig a fig, etc. We say, an honest man calls a spade a spade; and the French call "un chat un chat." Boileau says, "J'appelle un chat un chat, et Rolet un fripon."

{57b} Herodotus's history is comprehended in nine books, to each of which is prefixed the name of a Muse; the first is called Clio, the second Euterpe, and so on. A modern poet, I have been told, the ingenious Mr. Aaron Hill, improved upon this thought, and christened (if we may properly so call it), not his books, but his daughters by the same poetical names of Miss Cli, Miss Melp-y, Miss Terps-y, Miss Urania, etc.

{58} Both Thucydides and Livy are reprehensible in this particular; and the same objection may be made to Thuanus, Clarendon, Burnet, and many other modern historians.

{59} How just is this observation of Lucian's, and at the same time how truly poetical is the image which he makes use of to express it! It puts us in mind of his rival critic Longinus, who, as Pope has observed, is himself the great sublime he draws.

{60} By this very just observation, Lucian means to censure all those writers—and we have many such now amongst us—who take so much pains to smooth and round their periods, as to disgust their readers by the frequent repetition of it, as it naturally produces a tiresome sameness in the sound of them; and at the same time discovers too much that laborious art and care, which it is always the author's business as much as possible to conceal.

{61} See Homer's "Iliad," bk. xiii., 1. 4.

{62a} The famous Lacedæmonian general. The circumstance alluded to is in Thucydides, bk. iv.

{62b} Gr. ομοχρονειτω, a technical term, borrowed from music, and signifying that tone of the voice which exactly corresponds with the instrument accompanying it.

{66a} A coarse fish that came from Pontus, or the Black Sea.—Saperdas advehe Ponto. See Pers. Sat. v. 1. 134.

{66b} Here doctors differ. Several of Thucydides's descriptions are certainly very long, many of them, perhaps, rather tedious.

{67} Lucian is rather severe on this writer. Cicero only says, De omnibus omnia libere palam dixit; he spoke freely of everybody. Other writers, however, are of the same opinion with our satirist with regard to him. See

Dions. Plutarch. Cornelius Nepos, etc.

{69} Alluding to the story of Diogenes, as related in the beginning.

{75} See Homer's "Odyssey."—The strange stories which Lucian here mentions may certainly be numbered, with all due deference to so great a name, amongst the nugæ canoræ of old Homer. Juvenal certainly considers them in this light when he says:—

Tam vacui capitis populum Phæaca putavit.

Some modern critics, however, have endeavoured to defend them.

{77} Here the history begins, what goes before may be considered as the author's preface, and should have been marked as such in the original.

{79} Among the Greek wines, so much admired by ancient Epicures, those of the islands of the Archipelago were the most celebrated, and of these the Chian wine, the product of Chios, bore away the palm from every other, and particularly that which was made from vines growing on the mountain called Arevisia, in testimony of which it were easy, if necessary, to produce an amphora full of classical quotations.

The present inhabitants of that island make a small quantity of excellent wine for their own use and are liberal of it to strangers who travel that way, but dare not, being under Turkish government, cultivate the vines well, or export the product of them.

{81a} In the same manner as Gulliver's island of Laputa.—From this passage it is not improbable but that Swift borrowed the idea.

{81b} The account which Lucian here gives us of his visit to the moon, perhaps suggested to Bergerac the idea of his ingenious work, called "A Voyage to the Moon."

{82a} *Equi vultures*, horse vultures; from ιππος, a horse: and γυψ, a vulture.

{82b} Lucian, we see, has founded his history on matter of fact. Endymion, we all know, was a king of Elis, though some call him a shepherd. Shepherd or king, however, he was so handsome, that the moon, who saw him sleeping on Mount Latmos, fell in love with him. This no orthodox heathen ever doubted: Lucian, who was a freethinker, laughs indeed at the tale; but has made him ample amends in this history by creating him emperor of the moon.

{83a} Modern astronomers are, I, think, agreed, that we are to the moon just the same as the moon is to us. Though Lucian's history may be false, therefore his philosophy, we see, was true (1780). (The moon is not habitable, 1887.)

{83b} This I am afraid, is not so agreeable to the modern system; our philosophers all asserting that the sun is not habitable. As it is a place, however, which we are very little acquainted with, they may be mistaken, and Lucian may guess as well as ourselves, for aught we can prove to the contrary.

{84} Horse ants, from ιππος, a horse; and μυρμηξ, an ant.

{85a} From λαχανον, *olus*, any kind of herb; and πτεπον, *penna*, a wing.

{85b} *Millii jaculatores*, darters of millet; millet is a kind of small grain.— A strange species of warriors!

{85c} *Alliis pugnantes*, garlic fighters: these we are to suppose threw garlic at the enemy, and served as a kind of stinkpots.

{85d} *Pulici sagittarii*, flea-archers.

{85e} *Venti cursores*, wind courser.

{86a} *Passeres glandium*, acorn sparrows.

{86b} *Equi grues*, horse-cranes.

{87a} Air-flies.

{87b} Gr. Ἀεροκορακες, air-crows; but as all crows fly through the air, I would rather read Ἀερκορδακες, which may be translated air-dancers, from κορδαξ, cordax, a lascivious kind of dance, so called.

{88a} Gr. Καυλομυκητες, *Caulo fungi*, stalk and mushroom men.

{88b} Gr. Κυνοβαλανοι, *cani glandacii*, acorn-dogs.

{88c} Gr. Νεφελοκενταυροι, *nubicentauri*, cloud-centaurs.

{88d} The reason for this wish is given a little farther on in the History.

{89} See Hom. Il. II.. 1, 459.

{90a} Some authors tell us that Sagittarius was the same as Chiron the centaur; others, that he was Crocus, a famous hunter, the son of Euphemia, who nursed the Muses, at whose intercession, he was, after his death, promoted to the ninth place in the Zodiac, under the name of Sagittarius.

{90b} The inhabitants of the moon.

{92} A good burlesque on the usual form and style of treaties.

{93} Gr. Πυρωνιδης, *ignens*, fiery, Φλογιος, flaming, Νυκτωρ, *nocturnus*, nightly, Μηναιος, *menstruus*, monthly, Πολυλαμπης, *multi lucius*, many lights. These all make good proper names in Greek, and sound magnificently, but do not answer so well in English. I have therefore preserved the original words in the translation.

{94} Here Lucian, like other story-tellers, is a little deficient in point of memory. If they eat, as he tells us, nothing but frogs, what use could they have for cheese?

{96} Of which we shall see an account in the next adventure.

{97} The city of Lamps.

{98a} The cloud cuckoo.

{98b} See his comedy of the Birds.

{104a} *Salsamentarii*: Salt-fish-men.

{104b} Triton-weasels.

{104c} Greek, καρκινοχειχες, *cancri-mani*, crab's hands.

{104d} *Thynno-cipites*, tunny-heads, *i.e.*, men with heads like those of the tunny-fish.

{105a} Greek, παγουραδοι, crab-men.

{105b} ψηττοποδες, sparrow-footed, from ψηττα, *passer marinus*.

{109} *Maris potor*, the drinker up of the sea. Æolocentaurus and Thalassopotes were, I suppose, two Leviathans.

{113} One of the fifty Nereids, or Sea-Nymphs; so called, on account of the fairness of her skin: from γαλα, gala, milk; of the milky island, therefore, she was naturally the presiding deity.

{114a} Tyro, according to Homer, fell in love with the famous river Enipeus, and was always wandering on its banks, where Neptune found her, covered her with his waves, and throwing her into a deep sleep, supplied the place of Enipeus. Lucian has made her amends, by bestowing one of his imaginary kingdoms upon her. His part of the story, however, is full as probable as the rest.

{114b} *Suberipedes*, cork-footed.

{116a} This description of the Pagan Elysium, or Island of the Blessed, is well drawn, and abounds in fanciful and picturesque imagery, interspersed with strokes of humour and satire. The second book is, indeed, throughout, more entertaining and better written than the first.

{116b} See the Ajax Flagellifer of Sophocles. Lucian humorously degrades him from the character of a hero, and gives him hellebore as a madman.

{118} It is not improbable but that Voltaire's El Dorado in his "Candide," might have been suggested to him by this passage.

{119} *I.e.* Their appearance is exactly like that of shadows made by the sun at noonday, with this only difference, that one lies flat on the ground, the other is erect, and one is dark, the other light or diaphanous. Our vulgar idea of ghosts, especially with regard to their not being tangible, corresponds with this of Lucian's.

{121a} A famous musician. Clemens Alexandrinus gives us a full account of him, to whom I refer the curious reader.

{121b} This poet, we are told, wrote some severe verses on Helen, for which he was punished by Castor and Pollux with loss of sight, but on making his recantation in a palinodia, his eyes were graciously restored to him. Lucian has affronted her still more grossly by making her run away with Cinyrus; but he, we are to suppose, being not over superstitious, defied the power of Castor and Pollux.

{122a} Nothing appears more ridiculous to a modern reader than the perpetual encomiums on the musical merit of swans and swallows, which we meet with in all the writers of antiquity. A proper account and explanation of this is, I think, amongst the desiderata of literature. There is an entertaining tract on this subject in the "Hist. de l'Acad." tom. v., by M. Morin.

{122b} Who ravished Cassandra, the daughter of Priam and priestess of Minerva, who sent a tempest, dispersed the Grecian navy in their return home, and sunk Ajax with a thunder-bolt.

{123a} A scholar of Pythagoras.

{123b} The second king of Rome.

{123c} One of the seven sages, but excepted against by Lucian, because he was king of Corinth and a tyrant.

{123d} See his Treatise "de Republica." His quitting Elysium, to live in his own republic, is a stroke of true humour.

{124a} Alluding to a passage in Hesiod already quoted.

{124b} Lucian laughs at the sceptics, though he was himself one of them.

{126} Death-games, or games after death, in imitation of wedding-games, funeral-games, etc.

{127a} The famous tyrant of Agrigentum, renowned for his ingenious contrivance of roasting his enemies in a brazen bull, and not less memorable for some excellent epistles, which set a wit and scholar together by the ears concerning the genuineness of them. See the famous contest between Bentley and Boyle.

{127b} Who sacrificed to Jupiter all the strangers that came into his kingdom. "Hospites violabat," says Seneca, "ut eorum sanguine pluviam eliceret, cujus penuria Ægyptus novem annis laboraverat." A most ingenious contrivance.

{128a} A king of Thrace who fed his horses with human flesh.

{128b} Scyron and Pityocamptes were two famous robbers, who used to seize on travellers and commit the most horrid cruelties upon them. They were slain by Theseus. See Plutarch's "Life of Theseus."

{128c} Where he ran away, but, as we are told, in very good company. See Diog. Laert. Strabo, etc.

{132} The Antipodes. We never heard whether Lucian performed this voyage. D'Ablancourt, however, his French translator, in his continuation of the "True History," has done it for him, not without some humour, though it is by no means equal to the original.

{135a} Voltaire has improved on this passage, and given us a very humorous account of "les Habitans de l'Enfer," in his wicked "Pucelle."

{135b} Who, the reader will remember, had just before run off with Helen.

{136a} Greek, υπνος, sleep.

{136b} As herald of the morn.

{136c} A root which, infused, is supposed to promote sleep, consequently very proper for the Island of Dreams.

"Not poppy, nor mandragora,
Nor all the drowsy syrups of the East,
Shall ever medicine thee to that sweet sleep
Which thou ow'dst yesterday."
See Shakespeare's "Othello."

{136d} Night wanderer.

{137a} Gr. νεγρητος, *inexperrectus*, unwaked or wakeful.

{137b} Gr. παννυχια, *pernox*, all night.

{137c} "Two portals firm the various phantoms keep;
Of ev'ry one; whence flit, to mock the brain,
Of wingéd lies a light fantastic train;
The gate opposed pellucid valves adorn,
And columns fair, encased with polished horn;
Where images of truth for passage wait."
See Pope's Homer's "Odyssey," bk. xix., 1. 637.
See also Virgil, who has pretty closely imitated his master.

{138a} Gr. ταραξιωνα τον ματαιογενους, *terriculum vanipori*: fright, the son of vain hope, or disappointment.

{138b} Gr. πλουτοκλεα τον φαντασιωνος, *divitiglorium*, the pride of riches —*i.e.*, arising from riches; son of phantasy, or deceit.

{138c} Gr. καρεωτιν, *gravi-somnem*, heavy sleep.

{141a} Nut sailors; or, sailors in a nut-shell.

{141b} Those who sailed in the gourds.

{147a} Cabalusa and Hydamardia are hard words, which the commentators confess they can make nothing of. Various, however, are the derivations, and numerous the guesses made about them. The English reader may, if he pleases, call them not improperly, especially the first, Cabalistic.

{147b} Which the reader will remember was given him by way of charm, on his departure from the Happy Island.

{148} Gr. ονοσκελεας, *asini-eruras*, ass-legged.

{149} The ensuing books never appeared. The "True History," like
—"the bear and fiddle,
Begins, but breaks off in the middle."

D'Ablancourt, as I observed above, has carried it on a little farther. There is still room for any ingenious modern to take the plan from Lucian, and improve upon it.

{153} The ancient Greek stadium is supposed to have contained a hundred and twenty-five geometrical paces, or six hundred and twenty-five Roman feet, corresponding to our furlong. Eight stadia make a geometrical, or Italian mile; and twenty, according to Dacier, a French league. It is observed, notwithstanding, by Guilletiere, a famous French writer, that the stadium was only six hundred Athenian feet, six hundred and four English feet, or a hundred and three geometrical paces.

The Greeks measured all their distances by stadia, which, after all we can discover concerning them, are different in different times and places.

{154} The Phœnicians, it is supposed, were the first sailors, and steered their course according to the appearance of the stars.

{155} Greek, ουρανιων, *cælicolæ*, Homer's general name for the gods.

{156} Ganymede, whom Jupiter fell in love with, as he was hunting on Mount Ida, and turning himself into an eagle, carried up with him to heaven. "I am sure," says Menippus's friend, archly enough, "you were not carried up there, like Ganymede, for your beauty."

{157a} "Icarus Icariis nomina fecit aquis." The story is too well known to stand in need of any illustration. This accounts for the title of Icaro-Menippus.

{157b} See Bishop Wilkins's "Art of Flying," where this ingenious contrivance of Menippus's is greatly improved upon. For a humorous detail of the many advantages attending this noble art, I refer my readers to the *Spectator*.

{159} Even Lucian's Menippus, we see, could not reflect on the works of God without admiration; but with how much more dignity are they considered by the holy Psalmist!—

"O praise the Lord of heaven, praise Him in the height. Praise Him, sun and moon; praise Him, all ye stars; praise the Lord upon earth, ye dragons and all deeps; fire and hail, snow and vapours, wind and storm fulfilling His word."—Psalm cxlviii.

{161} This was the opinion of Anaxagoras, one of the Ionic philosophers, born at Clazomene, in the first year of the seventieth Olympiad. See Plutarch and Diogenes Laert.

{162} Alluding to the doctrines of Plato and Aristotle.

{163a} This was the opinion of Democritus, who held that there were infinite worlds in infinite space, according to all circumstances, some of which are not only like to one another, but every way so perfectly and absolutely equal, that there is no difference betwixt them. See Plutarch, and Tully, Quest. Acad.

{163b} Empedocles, of Agrigentum, a Pythagorean; he held that there are two principal powers in nature, amity and discord, and that

"Sometimes by friendship, all are knit in one,
Sometimes by discord, severed and undone."
See Stanley's "Lives of the Philosophers."

{163c} Alluding to the doctrine of Pythagoras, according to whom, number is the principle most providential of all heaven and earth, the root of divine beings, of gods and demons, the fountain and root of all things; that which, before all things, exists in the divine mind, from which, and out of which, all things are digested into order, and remain numbered by an indissoluble series. The whole system of the Pythagoreans is at large explained and illustrated by Stanley. See his "Lives of Philosophers."

{164} See our author's "Auction of Lives," where Socrates swears by the dog and the plane-tree.

This was called the ορκος Ραδαμανθιος, or oath of Rhadamanthus, who, as Porphyry informs us, made a law that men should swear, if they needs must swear, by geese, dogs, etc. υπερ που μη τους θεους επι πασιν ονομαζω, that they might not, on every trifling occasion, call in the name of the gods. This is a kind of religious reason, the custom was therefore, Porphyry tells us, adopted by the wise and pious Socrates. Lucian, however, who laughs at everything here (as well as the place above quoted), ridicules him for it.

{165a} See Homer's "Odyssey," book ix. 1. 302. Pope translates it badly, "Wisdom held my hand."

Homer says nothing but—my mind changed.

{165b} One of the fables here alluded to is yet extant amongst those ascribed to Æsop, but that concerning the camel I never met with.

{166a} That part of Athens which was called the upper city, in opposition to the lower city. The Acropolis was on the top of a high rock.

{166b} Mountains near Athens.

{166c} A mountain between Geranea and Corinth.

{166d} A high mountain in Arcadia, to the west of Elis. Erymanthus another, bordering upon Achaia. Taygetus another, reaching northwards, to the foot of the mountains of Arcadia.

{167} See Homer's "Iliad," book xiii. 1. 4

{168} See note on this in a former dialogue.

{169} It is reported of Empedocles, that he went to Ætna, where he leaped into the fire, that he might leave behind him an opinion that he was a god, and that it was afterwards discovered by one of his sandals, which the fire cast up again, for his sandals were of brass. See Stanley's "Lives of the Philosophers." The manner of his death is related differently by different authors. This was, however, the generally received fable. Lucian, with an equal degree of probability, carries him up to the moon.

{170} See Homer's Odyssey, b. xvi. 1. 187. The speech of Ulysses to his son, on the discovery.

{171} When Empedocles is got into the moon, Lucian makes him swear by Endymion in compliment to his sovereign lady.

{172a} Agathocles.

{172b} Stratonice.

{173} Of Achilles. See the 18th book of the "Iliad."

{175a} Greek, ο χορηγος.

{175b} Sicyon was a city near Corinth, famous for the richness and felicity of its soil.

{176a} The famous Ager Cynurius, a little district of Laconia, on the confines of Argolis; the Argives and Spartans, whom it laid between, agreed to decide the property of it by three hundred men of a side in the field: the battle was bloody and desperate, only one man remaining alive, Othryades, the Lacedæmonian, who immediately, though covered with wounds, raised a trophy, which he inscribed with his own blood, to Jupiter Tropæus. This victory the Spartans, who from that time had quiet possession of the field, yearly celebrated with a festival, to commemorate the event.

{176b} A mountain of Thrace. Dion Cassius places it near Philippi. It was supposed to have abounded in golden mines in some parts of it.

{177} When Æacus was king of Thessaly, his kingdom was almost depopulated by a dreadful pestilence; he prayed to Jupiter to avert the distemper, and dreamed that he saw an innumerable quantity of ants creep out of an old oak, which were immediately turned into men; when he awoke the dream was fulfilled, and he found his kingdom more populous than ever; from that time the people were called Myrmidons. Such is the fable, which owed its rise merely to the name of Myrmidons, which it was supposed must come from μυρμηξ, an ant. To some such trifling circumstances as these we are indebted for half the fables of antiquity.

{178a} See Homer's "Iliad," book i. 1. 294.

{178b} This was the opinion of Anaxagoras, and is confirmed by the more accurate observations of modern philosophy.

{179} *See* Pope's Homer's "Odyssey," book x. 1. 113.

{180a} *I.e.* Such a countenance as he put on when he slew the rebellious Titans.

{180b} See Homer's "Odyssey," A. v. 170

{181} Otus and Ephialtes were two giants of an enormous size; some of the ancients, who, no doubt, were exact in their measurement, assure us that, at nine years old, they were nine cubits round, and thirty-six high, and grew in proportion, till they thought proper to attack and endeavour to dethrone Jupiter; for which purpose they piled mount Ossa and Pelion upon Olympus, made Mars prisoner, and played several tricks of this kind, till Diana, by artifice, subdued them, contriving, some way or other, to make them shoot their arrows against, and destroy each other, after which Jupiter sent them down to Tartarus. Some attribute to Apollo the honour of conquering them. This story has been explained, and allegorised, and tortured so many different ways, that it is not easy to unravel the foundation of it.

{182} Jupiter thought himself, we may suppose, much obliged to Phidias for the famous statue which he had made of him, and therefore, in return, complaisantly inquires after his family.

{183a} From Aratus.

{183b} A city of Elis, where there was a temple dedicated to Olympian Jupiter, and public games celebrated every fifth year.

{183c} A city of Thessaly, where there was a temple to Jove; this was likewise the seat of the famous oracle.

{183d} A goddess worshiped in Thrace. Hesychius says this was only another name for Diana. See Strabo.

{184} Alluding to his Republic, which probably was considered by Lucian and others as a kind of Utopian system.

{185a} See Homer's "Iliad," book xvi. 1. 250.

{185b} Of Elis, founder of the Sceptic sect, who doubted of everything. He flourished about the hundred and tenth Olympiad.

{187a} 'Ου γαρ σιτον εδουα', ου πινουσ' αιθοπα οινον.
"—Not the bread of man their life sustains,
Nor wine's inflaming juice supplies their veins."
See Pope's Homer's "Iliad," book v. 1. 425.

{187b} Greek, υποβεβρεγμενοι.

{187c} See the beginning of the second book of the "Iliad."

{188a} Apollo is always represented as *imberbis*, or without a beard, probably from a notion that Phoebus, or the sun, must be always young.

{188b} See Homer's "Iliad," book xviii. 1. 134.
{189} See Homer's "Iliad," book ii. 1. 238.
{190} Greek, θρεμματα, what Virgil calls, ignavum pecus.

Printed in Great Britain
by Amazon